THE GREAT
DOG
Disaster

Katie Davies

Illustrated by Hannah Shaw

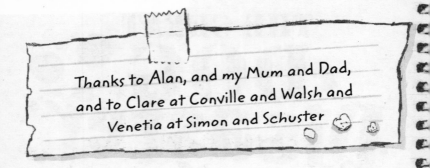

Thanks to Alan, and my Mum and Dad,
and to Clare at Conville and Walsh and
Venetia at Simon and Schuster

First published in Great Britain in 2012 by Simon and Schuster UK Ltd,
a CBS company.

Text copyright © 2012 Katie Davies
Cover and interior illustrations copyright © 2012 Hannah Shaw

The right of Katie Davies and Hannah Shaw to be identified as the author and illustrator of this
work respectively has been asserted by them in accordance with sections 77 and 78 of
the Copyright, Design and Patents Act, 1988.

Simon & Schuster UK Ltd
1st Floor, 222 Gray's Inn Road, London WC1X 8HB

A CIP catalogue record for this book is available from the British Library.

978-1-84738-598-7

3 5 7 9 10 8 6 4

Printed and bound in Great Britain by CPI Group (UK) Ltd, Croydon CR0 4YY

www.simonandschuster.co.uk
www.katiedaviesbooks.com

For the Davis boys, before you're all too big

MY VILLAGE
by Anna.

The Vet's

Cat Lady's House

church

to Aunt Deidra's House

Pet Shop

Sweet Shop

Railway Station

River

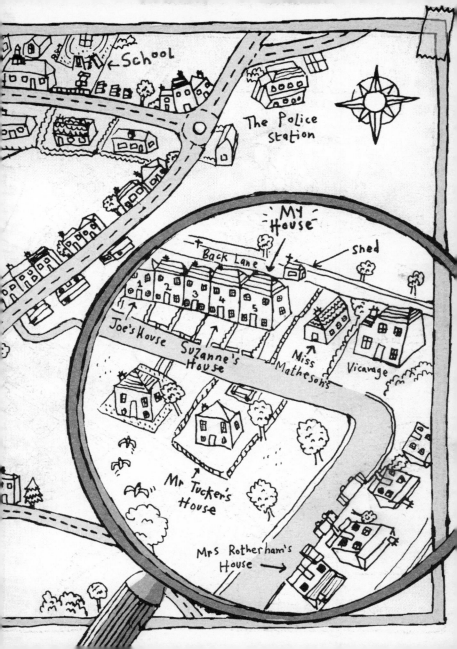

✾ CHAPTER 1 ✾
An Actual Disaster

This is a story about my friend Suzanne, and her dog, and me, and Tom, and the Great Dog Disaster. Most of the time, when people say, "Oh, it's a disaster!" it probably isn't. Like when Dad's watching football, and they're one nil up, and the whistle's going to go, and the keeper gets an own goal. Or when Mum's been to the shops, and put the bags in the boot, and slammed it shut, and locked the car keys inside it. Or when it's Mrs Constantine's Sunday

School Concert, and Emma Hendry starts her solo, and her hair gets set on fire by Graham Roberts' christingle candle. Those things might be bad (especially for Emma Hendry, because her hair had never been cut before and she had to have a bob), but they aren't actual disasters. Because I looked 'disaster' up, in my dictionary, and this is what it said . . .

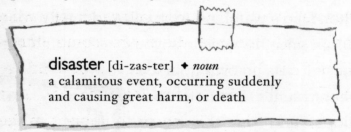

disaster [di-zas-ter] ✦ *noun*
a calamitous event, occurring suddenly
and causing great harm, or death

The Great Dog Disaster *was* an Actual Disaster though. It got on the news, and in the paper, and me and Tom and Suzanne had our photos taken and everything.

Tom is my brother. He's five. He's four years younger than me. I'm nine. My name is Anna. I've got another brother and a sister too, but they're not in this story because they're older than me and Tom and they don't really care about dogs, and disasters, and things that me and Suzanne do. Anyway, even though lots of people have heard about the Great Dog Disaster, it's only me who knows exactly what happened. Because there are some things about it that I have never told anyone. And I'm going to put those in this story as well. And when it's finished I'll put my notebook in the shed, on the shelf, where no one will see it, behind the worms, and the wasp trap, and the piccalilli jar that's got all Suzanne's stitches in.

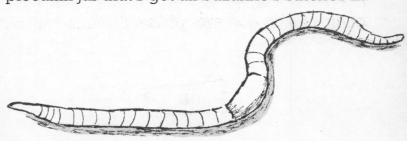

CHAPTER 2
The Guillotine

Suzanne lives next door. Her surname is Barry. Mine and Suzanne's bedrooms are right next to each other. The wall between our house and the Barrys' house is so thin that if you put your ear against the wall in our house, you can hear all the things the Barrys' are doing on their side. When Mum sees me with my ear against the wall, she says, "For goodness' sake, Anna, can't you think of anything better to do than eavesdropping on next door?"

And I say, "No." Because if I *could* think of something better to do, I would have done that in the first place. Listening in on the Barrys is pretty good  because you hear lots of things, like when it's time for lunch, and whether it's lentil soup, and how afterwards Suzanne's Dad can't come out of the toilet, and if Suzanne's that desperate she'll have to,

'GO IN THE GARDEN!'

Anyway, like I told Mum, I'm not the only one that eavesdrops. Because Suzanne listens in on *us* from her side of the wall as well. And in the morning, when we're walking to school, we tell each other all the things we heard happen through the wall the night before.

Me and Suzanne don't just listen through the wall. We talk through it too. It's not that easy talking through a wall, unless you shout, but me and Suzanne can't do that because most of the things we need to say are secrets. We've tried millions of ways of talking through the wall. We put them on a list and pinned it up in the shed. The shed is out the back, in the lane, and only me and Suzanne are allowed to go in it. Except Tom, when he wants to, but most of the time he's busy doing other things, like talking to Mr Tucker, or collecting gravel, or trying to walk in a straight line with his eyes closed.

ANNA'S AND SUZANNE'S LIST OF ALL THE WAYS WE HAVE TRIED FOR TALKING THROUGH THE WALL AND WHY WE HAD TO STOP AND TRY SOMETHING ELSE INSTEAD

WAY FOR TALKING THROUGH THE WALL:	WHY IT DIDN'T WORK:
Dig a tunnel through the wall to join our bedrooms together	Suzanne's Dad looked under her bed, and saw where we had started digging, and banned us from Suzanne's bedroom
Climb out of our bedroom windows and sit on our window ledges and talk out there	Mum got bolts put into our window frames, and now we can't open them wide enough to climb out

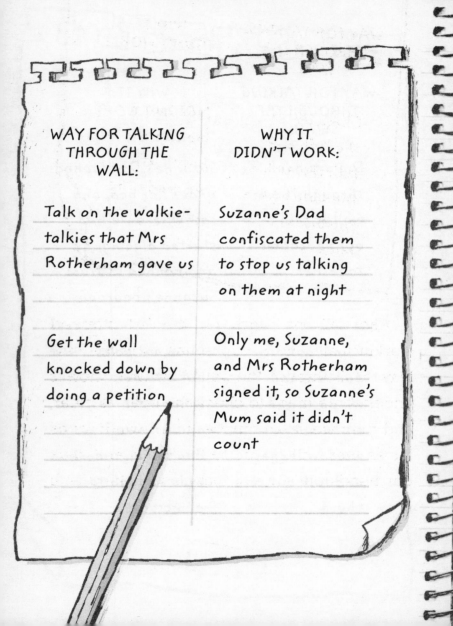

WAY FOR TALKING THROUGH THE WALL:	WHY IT DIDN'T WORK:
Talk on the walkie-talkies that Mrs Rotherham gave us	Suzanne's Dad confiscated them to stop us talking on them at night
Get the wall knocked down by doing a petition	Only me, Suzanne, and Mrs Rotherham signed it, so Suzanne's Mum said it didn't count

WAY FOR TALKING THROUGH THE WALL:	WHY IT DIDN'T WORK:
Climb up in the loft, and talk through the hole where the bricks are missing	Mum put a lock on the loft hatch after we made the ceiling fall in

After all the ways on the list stopped working, me and Suzanne had to find a new way to talk through the wall. What we do now is knock three times to check the coast is clear, and then we open our bedroom windows as far as they will go, up to the bolts, and stick our heads out. It's not that good talking with your head hanging out of the window. Because you have to bend right over, and the window frame digs into your neck, and if it's raining your head gets wet. When Mrs Rotherham walked past and saw me and Suzanne with our heads sticking out, she said, "Hello up there. You girls look as though you're about to be guillotined. Beautiful morning for it!"

I know all about guillotines because we did them at school with Mrs Peters. This is what it says a guillotine is in my dictionary...

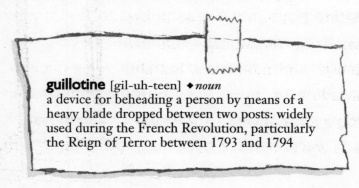

guillotine [gil-uh-teen] ◆ *noun*
a device for beheading a person by means of a heavy blade dropped between two posts: widely used during the French Revolution, particularly the Reign of Terror between 1793 and 1794

Mrs Rotherham is really old. If she was French she would probably have seen people getting guillotined herself. Because everyone in France went to watch. Especially the old ladies. They did their knitting while they waited for the heads to get chopped off.

Mrs Rotherham lives up the road. She was Nanna's friend, before Nanna died. Her house smells a bit strange. Of old things, and mothballs. But she always asks you in, and gives you ice cream, and she never tells you not to do things.

Anyway, after Mrs Rotherham said we looked like we were in a guillotine, me and Suzanne started pretending that we were, and saying things in French, like "bonjour" and "zut alors", and "OFF WIZ ZER 'EADS!" And making the sound of the blades dropping down. And Suzanne pulls her head inside so it looks like it's been sliced off. And I scream, and make choking sounds and pretend my guillotine's gone wrong, and my head's still hanging on. Only I have to do it quietly, because if Mum hears she comes in and says, "Don't play guillotines please, girls. It's not a good game." (Which isn't actually true, because it *is* a good game and, like Suzanne said, Mum wouldn't know because she's probably never played it.)

Sometimes, when we're in the guillotine,

me and Suzanne can see Mr Tucker opposite.
Mr Tucker is old as well. Even older than Mrs
Rotherham. He was in The War. Flying planes,
and fighting, and blowing stuff up and all that.
Mr Tucker doesn't fly planes anymore. Apart
from pretend ones with Tom. Most of the time
he just goes up and down the road, picking up
the litter, and checking how much rain there
is in his rain gauge and spotting what kind the
clouds are.

☙ CHAPTER 3 ☙

A Hairy Heirloom

The day before Suzanne got her dog, I listened in on the Barrys a lot. Normally, when I wake up on weekends, I do stuff with Tom. Like helping him line up his stones, or finding him things to fix with his Bob the Builder tool kit, or counting how long he can hold his breath before he falls over. Because if you knock on Suzanne's wall, and ring the bell, and shout, **"IS *ANYBODY THERE?*"** through the letterbox, before the Barrys' curtains are open, Suzanne's Dad runs down in his pants, and opens the letterbox from the inside, and says, **"IT'S 6.45 ON A SUNDAY! ARE YOU OUT**

OF **YOUR MIND?"** Suzanne's Dad always shouts. You don't need to put your ear against the wall to hear *him*.

Anyway, this Sunday, Suzanne's Dad was up early, and he wasn't happy, because I could hear him through the wall, saying, **"WHAT?"** and **"YOU MUST BE JOKING?"** and **"I CAN'T BELIEVE WHAT I'M HEARING HERE!"**

So I left Tom in the hall, holding his breath, and I went to the kitchen, where the shouting was loudest. Mum was there, standing still, staring at the wall.

"Are you listening in on the Barrys?"

Mum jumped. "No."

"Oh."

"I'm making a cup of tea actually."

I didn't think Mum *was* making a cup of tea,

because the kettle wasn't on, and she hadn't got a teabag out, or a cup, but I didn't say anything because I needed to listen in.

"NO, NO, NO!" Suzanne's Dad said, **"I DON'T NEED TO DISCUSS IT, BRIDGET."** Bridget is Suzanne's Mum's name. **"WE ARE DEFINITELY NOT GETTING A DOG!"**

But Mum turned the tap on, and filled the kettle, and started clanking about in the cup cupboard. "That's enough eavesdropping. Find something else to do, please, Big Ears."

So I went upstairs to knock for Suzanne. On the way I saw Tom. He was leaning against the wall in the hall, making a moaning sound. His head was bright red, like it was about to burst. "And… stop!" I said.

Tom breathed out, and fell down. "Phew!

How long did I do?"

"Urm... a hundred and twenty seconds," I told him, which it probably wasn't, because I'd forgotten to keep count, and that's how long most grown-ups can hold their breath, and Tom's only five and he's the smallest in his class.

Tom was pretty pleased. "That's the best ever," he said. "I better get a biscuit." After holding his breath, and spotting what kind the clouds are with Mr Tucker, eating biscuits is Tom's best thing.

I went upstairs to my bedroom, and knocked three times on the wall. Suzanne knocked back. We stuck our heads out of our windows. "Bonjour," I said.

"Bonjour."

"What was your Dad shouting about before?"

23

"I'm not supposed to say."

"Oh," I said. And I didn't ask again because whenever Suzanne says she's not supposed to tell you something, she really just wants you to ask "Why?" a million times, and say, "oh *please*, go *on*, I won't tell anyone..." And the more you ask, the longer she makes you wait. So I just coughed, and made a clicking noise with my tongue, and picked a bit of paint off the window ledge.

And after ages, Suzanne said, "Alright then, I'll tell you. Meet me at the shed. Zey 'ave pardoned us from ze guillotine zis time."

Suzanne's good at French. She's got a dictionary that says 'French-English, English-French' on the front.

We put the lock on the shed door. And

made up a password. And Suzanne told me all about what was happening in her house. And how her Mum had an aunt, called Deidra, who she hadn't seen in ages, even though she lived nearby, because of Aunt Deidra being on the side of the family that Suzanne's Gran didn't speak to. And how Aunt Deidra's Nephew, Mick, had left a message on their machine, saying that Aunt Deidra had died, and had left something behind for Suzanne's Mum in her will.

This is what it says a 'will' is in my dictionary.

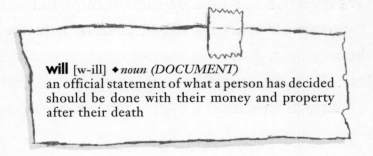

will [w-ill] ◆ *noun (DOCUMENT)*
an official statement of what a person has decided should be done with their money and property after their death

"Anyway," Suzanne said, "Dad hoped Great Aunt Deidra had left Mum some diamonds. But she hadn't. It's something much better. You'll never guess what it is."

"Is it her dog?"

"Oh," Suzanne said. "Yes. It is." And she didn't look very pleased. Because she probably wanted to make me guess the answer for ages. And say, "Nope. Guess again." Like she normally does.

Anyway, Suzanne's Dad wasn't happy about the dog. He said he wouldn't have it in the house.

"We need to do something to make Dad change his mind."

I didn't think there was much point in trying to make Suzanne's Dad change his mind. Because for one thing Suzanne's Dad is allergic to dogs. They make his nose run and his eyes itch and his face puff right up. And that's why he sent Suzanne's old dog, Barney, to live on a farm, where he can roam free in the fields, and he's much better off.

And for another thing he had already said, **"NO."** Three times. In a row. Really loud. Because I heard him through the wall. And for an even other thing Suzanne's Dad's not the kind of person who does change his mind. Especially not about dogs. Because Suzanne has tried to make him get another dog before. About a million times.

"But this time is different, because we have been *given* a dog," Suzanne said, "by a *dead* person." And she said we should do a list of reasons why getting Great Aunt Deidra's dog was a good idea. And give it to her Dad. So that's what we did. Because Suzanne's not the sort of person who changes her mind, either.

ANNA'S AND SUZANNE'S LIST OF REASONS WHY THE BARRYS SHOULD GET DEAD AUNT DEIDRA'S DOG

1. The dog can live in the garage, and never even come in the house at all (except on its birthday. And at Christmas. And then Suzanne's Dad can take tablets called anti-histamines, like Emma Hendry has at school, for when she goes too near the guinea-pig).

2. The dog can guard against burglars.

3. The dog can stop the New Cat from coming into the garden and hiding by the bird table, and killing all the Blue Tits (the New Cat is our cat. It's not that new anymore but that's still what it's called. We got it wild, off a farm, after the Old Cat died. Nobody likes it. Except Tom.)

4. Suzanne will take the dog for two walks every day, and feed it, and train it, and pick up all its poos. And no one else will have to do anything.

5. If she is allowed the dog, Suzanne will never ask for anything else again. Ever. And especially not any more dogs. And, if she does, the dog can go back to Aunt Deidra's Nephew, Mick.

When the list was finished, Suzanne took it home to read to her Dad. I went into our kitchen and put my ear against the wall.

"I'm not interested," Suzanne's Dad said, before Suzanne had even started.

Suzanne read the list anyway. Then she waited. "Well?"

"Well *what?*"

"*Now* do you think it's a good idea to get the dog?"

"NO!"

"Oh."

"I'M GOING TO COUNT TO THREE, SUZANNE, AND IF YOU'RE STILL HERE.... *ONE, TWO...*"

Suzanne ran upstairs.

I kept my ear against the wall. Suzanne's Mum came into their kitchen.

"DON'T START, BRIDGET!"

"I wasn't going to."

"GOOD."

"It's just it was poor Aunt Deidra's *dying wish*…"

"YOU HADN'T SEEN YOUR AUNT DEIDRA IN YEARS!"

"All the more reason to have her dog now she's dead."

And then Mum came into the kitchen and started going on about not eavesdropping again. And last week's swimming things. And how I had to take them out of the bag, because if my costume went mouldy again I wasn't getting another one.

"Shh," I said, "You're making me miss what's happening in

31

Suzannes's house."

Then Suzanne's Dad said,

"IT'S MY HEALTH AND HAPPINESS OR THIS DAMN DOG'S. YOU DECIDE!"

And the Barrys' front door slammed. And their car started. And went off down the road. And everything went quiet.

And Suzanne shouted through the wall,

"WE'RE GETTING DEAD AUNT DEIDRA'S DOG!"

CHAPTER 4
Lifesavers

The next day was Monday. And, apart from being the day that Suzanne's Great Aunt Deidra's Dog was coming, nothing was different. Me and Suzanne woke up like normal. And walked to school together like normal. And sat at our desks, like normal. And everything was just like it always is. Except longer. Because that's what happens when you're waiting for something. After school, me and Suzanne went swimming like we normally do on a Monday. The swimming lesson we go to isn't a normal swimming lesson, though. Because, like Sandra, who's in charge, says,

"You want to splash about, drift up and down, fanny around with floats? You've come to the wrong class, my friend. Try Water Wingers on Wednesdays. This is Lifesavers. Where swimming gets serious. There's nothing funny about subaqueous asphyxiation."

Which is true. This is what it says subaqueous is in my dictionary...

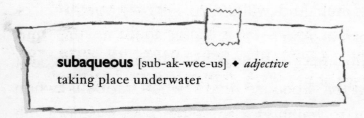

subaqueous [sub-ak-wee-us] ◆ *adjective*
taking place underwater

And this is what it says about asphyxiation ...

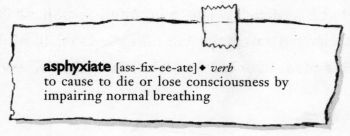

asphyxiate [ass-fix-ee-ate] ◆ *verb*
to cause to die or lose consciousness by impairing normal breathing

Suzanne didn't used to be allowed to go swimming. Because of her grommets. But now that she's had them taken out, she can. Suzanne keeps her grommets in an old piccalilli jar, with her adenoids and her stitches, on the shelf in the shed. She used to keep them on the shelf in her kitchen, until her Dad tried to put them in his cheese sandwich.

"Hey!" Suzanne said, "my adenoids!"

Suzanne's Dad threw them in the bin. **"WHO KEEPS OLD BODY PARTS IN WITH THE CONDIMENTS, FOR CRYING OUT LOUD?!"**

And Suzanne had to fish them out.

Anyway, it's pretty good at Lifesavers, better than Brownies, because you don't have to do a sewing badge, or skip three times round a toadstool, or promise to serve the Queen. You dive to the bottom of the pool in your pyjamas to get bricks back, and throw ropes out into the water, and do Real-Life Rescues on Darren the Resuscitation Dummy. And sometimes Sandra says, "It's bad weather", and she puts the wave machine on, and the freezing cold hose, and runs up and down the side of the pool, blowing her whistle, and shouting through the loudspeaker, **"QUICK!"** and, **"HE'S GOING UNDER!"** and, **"TEN MORE SECONDS AND HE'LL BE BRAIN DEAD!"** Which makes it even better.

Anyway, the day Great Aunt Deidra's Dog was coming, after we had practised speed swimming, and taken it in turns to pump water out of Darren the Resuscitation

Dummy's lungs, it was time to try Real-Life Rescues.

Sandra blew her whistle. "***Fweeeeeeet!*** Everyone out, on the side. Let's see these Open Water Rescue Skills in action. The situation is this: Emma Hendry and Darren are having a picnic by a lake. The sun is shining. The birds are singing. What could possibly go wrong? But wait..." She pointed to the deep end. "The ground around the lake is wet, slippery still from last night's rain. Darren's a non-swimmer. Isn't he dangerously close to the edge? What about Emma's footwear? Is it appropriate? Anna Morris and Suzanne Barry, you're out walking nearby. Is that a splash you hear?" She blew her whistle again. "**Fweeeeeet!** Positions, people!"

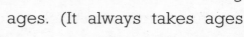

Me and Suzanne went round the corner, into the changing room, and waited. And Emma spread an imaginary blanket on the ground, and sat Darren the Resuscitation Dummy down on it, and started putting out the picnic and saying, "Well, this is nice…" and, "just the two of us, Darren…" and "cheese savoury sandwich?" Which was taking ages. (It always takes ages with Emma.

She's in the school Drama Group. And that's why sometimes Sandra shouts **"MOVE IT ALONG, HENDRY. THIS IS AN _EMERGENCY_, NOT AN EPISODE OF EASTENDERS!"**). Anyway, while we were waiting for Emma to fall in the water, me and Suzanne started talking about Great Aunt Deidra's Dog, and all the things we were going to do with it. Like race it up the road, and teach it tricks, and put it on an obstacle course, with cones and hoops and jumps, and all that. And Suzanne said we needed to decide on a name. And she told me the ones at the top of her list, like Cheetah, and Blaze, and Ace, and Bullet. And we forgot about the lake, for a bit, and listening out for a

splash. And then we heard, "HELP!"

We ran out of the changing room. Emma was thrashing around in the deep end. Suzanne grabbed the rescue rope from the hook on the wall. "Stand back!" She threw it out, across the water, to the other side of the pool. "Grab hold!" The rope landed right next to Emma's hand. Suzanne pulled her into the side, and we dragged her out of the water, and I wrapped her in the imaginary picnic blanket and put her in the recovery position.

Emma shivered, "D-D-D-Darren, help Darren . . ."

Suzanne dived in. I went after her. Darren was lying on his back at the bottom of the pool.

40

We tried to pull him up but he'd already filled with water.

"*Fweeeet!*" Sandra blew her whistle.

I came back up. "He's too heavy."

Suzanne came up for air. "We need more time."

"You're too late, ladies. Darren has been submerged for sixteen minutes."

"He might still be alive," I said. "Because Peter Colat from Switzerland is. And he once held his breath underwater for nineteen minutes, and twenty-one seconds."

"Peter Colat is a professional freediver and world record holder, Anna. Darren's never even done his five metres."

41

"If only he'd told me he couldn't swim," Emma said. "I wouldn't have sat him so close to the edge…"

Sandra fished Darren out with the long pole with the hook on the end, and laid him face down on the side. "Darren has *had it*."

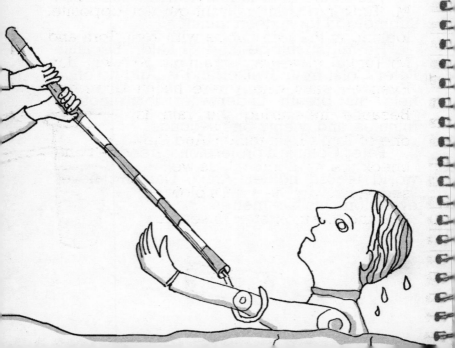

❝ CHAPTER 5 ❞
The Rain Gauge

After we got back from Lifesavers, and had our tea, me and Suzanne sat down on the path outside Suzanne's house, and waited for Great Aunt Deidra's Nephew to bring the dog. Mr Tucker was in his front garden, opposite, looking in the rain gauge with Tom. Tom and Mr Tucker measure the rain gauge every day. Even on days when there hasn't been any. Because measuring the rain is one of Tom's best things. And they check the weathercock as well, to see which way the wind's blowing. And the thermometer, to see how

hot it is. "Two millimetres of the old wet stuff today, Tom. What do you say, eh, Popsie?" Mr Tucker always calls me Popsie, even though, like I've told him, it's not my name.

I didn't say anything because I don't like talking to Mr Tucker about the weather much, because it always takes ages, and sometimes he gets his logbook out, and that's got graphs in.

"We're waiting for a dog," Suzanne said. And she told Mr Tucker about her Mum's Aunt Deidra, and how she had died, and left her dog behind.

"Sounds like a fine woman, this Deidra," Mr Tucker said. "Black do, her dying. Great Aunts have a habit of it. Damned nasty business.

44

Used to have one myself. Great Aunt Eida. Six sons, until four of them went in The War. Crippled with arthritis, but walked Hadrian's Wall in a one-piece for Multiple Sclerosis and made marvellous mince pies. Still, a dog, eh, Blondie?''

Mr Tucker always calls Suzanne Blondie, even though her hair is brown.

''What do you say, Basher?''

Tom said he hoped this dog didn't jump up, like Barney used to. Or lick. Or chase after the New Cat.

''It probably will,'' Suzanne said. ''Because that's what dogs *do*.''

''You have to be careful with cats,'' Tom said. Which is true. Apart from with the New Cat. Because it was a wild cat, off a farm. And it's not scared of anything. Especially not dogs. It's not scared of Miss Matheson's dog anyway. Miss Matheson lives next door to us, on the other side to Suzanne. Her dog is the same size as a guinea-pig. It fits in her handbag. It runs up and down all day on the other side of Miss Matheson's fence, and yaps and snaps, and if anyone comes close, it attacks.

"I shall take a shufti at this dog myself, of course, give it the old once over. Debrief, the animal, eh, Basher, that make you feel better?" And Tom said that would make him feel better, and *another* thing that would make him feel better was a biscuit.

Mr Tucker took Tom indoors, to see if he could find one.

CHAPTER 6
Dead Aunt Deidra's Dog

The car stopped outside Suzanne's house. A big man with a small T-shirt on opened the door and got out. Suzanne's Mum came out of the house to meet him.

"Mick? Bridget. It must be ten years. You haven't changed a bit."

"Humph."

"I hope you won't find the dog too hard to part with."

"Not *too* hard."

Mick went to the back door. Where me and Suzanne were looking

through the window. There was something black and furry lying across the back seat. It looked like the black sheepskin rug Mrs Rotherham has in front of her fire. Mick opened the door. And stepped back to let us see. The furry thing stayed still.

"Is it asleep?" Suzanne asked.

Suzanne's Mum opened the door opposite, and stuck her head inside. "Well, hello…*oh*." She covered her mouth. "What on *earth* is that smell?"

"Dog doesn't like cars," Mick said.

"Phew. I've never smelt anything *like* it."

I stuck my head in the car and sniffed. "I have," I said. Which was true. Because it smelled like Mrs Peter's class, the time Graham Roberts brought a dead vole in, in his

PE bag, and left it all week on his peg.

Mick leant in and gave the fur a shake. "We're here, wake up!"

Two small brown eyes opened. They were bloodshot and a bit misty, like Nanna's used to be, before she had her operation. The eyes looked up at Great Aunt Deidra's Nephew, and blinked, then they closed again.

"It's gone back to sleep," I said.

"Come on, dog, jump down," Suzanne's

Mum patted her knees. "You'll feel better out in the air." The dog stayed still.

"Doesn't like to move, much, either," Mick said, "that's why I came in the car. Would've taken all week, walking."

Suzanne's Mum clapped her hands. "That's it, down you come." The dog still didn't budge.

Mr Tucker came out of his house with Tom, and crossed over to the car. He gave Great Aunt Deidra's Nephew the salute. "Wing Commander Raymond Tucker, six one seven squadron."

Aunt Deidra's Nephew kept his hand in his pocket. "Mick."

"Black do about your Aunt. I had an Aunt myself. Wonderful woman—"And he started telling Suzanne's Great Aunt Deidra's Nephew about his Aunt Eida's six sons, and the four that died, and her mince pies and all that.

"Where's the dog?" Tom asked.

Aunt Deidra's Nephew pointed to the back seat. The dog was lying flat on its back with its head hanging over the edge.

"Is it dead?"

"No," Suzanne said. "It's not."

"It won't come out," I said.

"It will. You just have to ask it right." Suzanne knows a lot about dogs because of Barney, and his training classes, and from her book called *You and Your Dog: Training and Tricks*. She held up her finger, and looked the dog in the eye, and said, "Come!" in her special dog training voice. The dog didn't do anything. She said it again, slow, like a warning, "*Come*..." The dog looked back at Suzanne and blinked.

"Maybe it's deaf," I said.

"It's not deaf," Suzanne said.

"Frozen on the stick, eh?" Mr Tucker stuck his head inside in the car too. "Ahem, bit ripe in here, harrumph..." One of the dog's ears went up. "Now then, look lively, it's a simple op, dog. On three, my count, think of Aunt Deidra, and bail out. One, two, three..." The dog didn't move. "That's it. You've got the green. Chocks away..." The dog stayed still. "Now, that's a direct order, dog. Let's not play silly beggars."

"The only way to shift it is to give it a swift kick," Mick said.

"No need for rough house. Must be some other way to clear it out of the old land creeper here, eh?"

"We could get in a long line and pull it out, like in *The Enormous Turnip*," Tom said. *The Enormous Turnip* is one of Tom's best books.

Suzanne made her eyes go up, like she does when she thinks you've said something

stupid, and she started telling Tom how getting a dog out of a car isn't the same as getting a turnip out of the ground, because of dogs being different to turnips and all that.

But Mr Tucker butted in. "Spot on, Basher. *Enormous Turnip* it is. Righto, wing, get weaving."

And he got us all in a line, in order of height. Apart from Great Aunt Deidra's Nephew, because he said he had a bad back.

Mr Tucker held onto the dog's collar, and Suzanne's Mum held onto Mr Tucker, and I held onto Suzanne's Mum. And Suzanne held onto me, and Tom held onto Suzanne.

"That's it, wing. Stand to. Take the strain..." Mr Tucker said. "Steady ... *Pull* ..." The dog slid out of the car and slopped onto the street.

And Great Aunt Deidra's Nephew got back
in the car and said goodbye, and drove off,
quick.

CHAPTER 7

The New Cat

The dog got up on its feet.

"It's big," Tom said. And it was. It had a big head, and big legs and a big body. It was the biggest dog I had ever seen.

"It could be a *bear*."

"It isn't a bear," Suzanne said.

"It *looks* like one," said Tom.

Which was true. It did. And not a very happy one.

"Like one of those dancing bears that have to stand on hot coals in Siberia, and get kept in cages," I said.

"No it doesn't," Suzanne said. But it did.

Because I've seen them. On TV.

"Maybe we should keep *this* one in a cage," Tom said, "in case it's the kind of *bear dog* that jumps up, and licks, and goes after the New Cat."

"It's not going in a cage," Suzanne said.

Mr Tucker pointed up the road. "Speak of the devil..."

The New Cat was sitting on Miss Matheson's wall, with its eyes all wide, and its fur all up, staring down at the dog.

Suzanne grabbed the dog's collar, "*Staaay* . . . " and pulled against it, like it was trying to get away.

The New Cat jumped down and started walking towards it, all

low down to the ground, like it does when it's hunting. And when it got close, it arched its back and hissed. "*Tssss.*"

Great Aunt Deidra's dog breathed in, and opened its jaws, wider and wider, showing its great big teeth.

"It's going to eat the New Cat!" Tom said. The New Cat's whiskers twitched. The dog's teeth snapped shut in front of the New Cat's nose. It stretched.

"What a *yawn*," said Mr Tucker.

The dog turned round, in a circle, and lay down, and closed its eyes. The New Cat sat still for a

bit, and waited. Then it turned around, and put its tail in the air, and walked off up the road.

"It's not the kind of bear-dog that goes after cats," said Tom.

Suzanne's Mum laughed. "This dog's cat-catching days are over."

"Is it old?" Tom asked.

"Ooh, yes."

"It could catch cats," said Suzanne. "If it wanted." The dog started to snore.

"Quite right," said Mr Tucker. "Dog's in its prime. Just like I am." He stretched. And rubbed his back. "What are we calling her when she's at home?"

"I thought Cheetah," Suzanne said, "or Blaze, or Bullet."

Suzanne's Mum felt around the dog's collar.

"I think she already has a name." She showed Suzanne a tag.

Suzanne read it. "Sorrel Cottage."

"No, that's where Aunt Deidra lived. Turn it around. What does the other side say?"

"It says *Beatrice*," Suzanne said. And she didn't look very pleased.

CHAPTER 8
Walkies

After Mr Tucker went home for his tea, and Suzanne's Mum went in to give baby Carl his bath, and Tom went to ask Mum for a biscuit, Suzanne decided it was time to take Beatrice for a walk.

"I don't think Beatrice is *that* old, do you, Anna?"

I looked at Beatrice. She was still asleep in the road. Her eyes were all droopy, and runny, with crusty stuff in the corners, and there were lumps, like warts, in her eyebrows, and her mouth sagged down, and her tongue hung out, and her teeth were brown, and there was a line of dribble from her lips, and her fur had matted patches, and there were other places where it was missing, and she smelt like Graham Roberts' P.E. bag with the dead vole, at her back end. And at the front she smelt like Mrs Constantine's pond, the time it went green with slime and the fish all floated to the top.

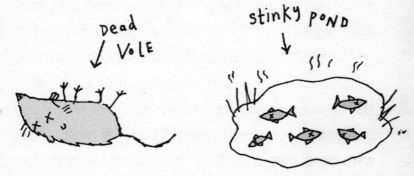

Dead Vole

stinky POND

"It's hard to tell with dogs," I said. Because *people* have lots of things to show how old they are, like Mrs Rotherham's got a walking stick,

and two pairs of glasses on a chain around her neck that she swaps over all the time, and enormous pants like cycling shorts that she hangs on the line. But dogs don't have any of those things.

"Beatrice might not even be old at all," Suzanne said. "She might just be tired because she probably hasn't been sleeping well, staying at Mick's house. And once she's been out for a W.A.L.K. she'll start sniffing around, and jumping up, and chasing after cats when they come near like proper dogs do."

I said I thought that Suzanne was right, because she normally is, about most things, and especially about dogs.

"I'll go and get the L.E.A.D. and some S.N.A.C.K.S."

Suzanne always spells out 'lead' instead of saying it, and 'walk', and 'snacks' as well, because, when she had Barney, before he went to live on the farm, to roam free, where he's better off, if he heard those words, he went mad, and ran round in circles, and jumped up and sent Suzanne flying.

Suzanne came back out, jangling the lead. "*Beatrice*..." Beatrice carried on snoring. Suzanne bent down and lifted up one of the dog's ears, "Beatrice?" Beatrice opened one eye. She looked at Suzanne, and she looked at the lead. "Walkies." Beatrice put her chin on her paws and closed her eye again.

"Maybe Beatrice doesn't like walks."

Suzanne made her eyes go up. "*All* dogs like walks, Anna." She clipped the lead onto Beatrice's collar and gave it a little tug. Then she gave it a bigger tug. Then she put it over her shoulder. "*Uungh*…you'll like it once you get going, Beatrice." And pulled as hard as she could. Beatrice didn't budge. "You'll have to push, Anna."

I wasn't sure Beatrice *would* like it once she got going, because that's what Mum always used to tell me about Brownies. And I never did. Apart from once, when she brought Tom with her to pick me up. And he ran in, in the middle of Shelly Wainwright's Promise Ceremony, and skipped around the toadstool and said his name was Rumpelstiltskin. I went behind Beatrice and pushed anyway. Her fur was greasy, and matted, and underneath it I could feel her bones.

"And *again*," Suzanne said.

I pushed harder.

"What if you got right underneath her, with your shoulder, and leaned in close, and pushed forwards and up like a lever…"

I didn't really want to get underneath Beatrice with my shoulder and push up like a lever, because that would mean my face would be right in Beatrice's bum. And I don't like putting my face in dogs' bums much, and especially not in old dogs' bums, like Beatrice's, which have greasy hair, and bald bits, and matted lumps, and smell of a dead vole that's been in a P.E. bag for a week.

"What about if we swap places and *I* hold the lead and pull, and *you* get down under Beatrice's bum and lever her up?"

"No," Suzanne said. "Because I'm the one that knows all about dogs and training, and what to say, and how to say it, like 'sit' and 'stay' and 'heel' and all that. And if we start swapping around, Beatrice will get confused."

So I got down on the ground, and took a deep breath, and held it, and wriggled my shoulder underneath Beatrice's bum.

"Ready?" Suzanne asked.

I nodded.

"Three, two, one... *Lift-off.*"

I closed my eyes and pushed forward and up as hard as I could, and tried to think about something else. My arms shook.

"Push, Anna."

"Nngnngya!"

"That's it."

Beatrice's back end wobbled a bit, and lifted, until she was up on her feet.

"There." Suzanne said, "Easy." I didn't say anything. Because I was lying on the ground, in the gravel, getting Beatrice's hairs out of my mouth.

We started off down the road on our walk. It was slow. Even slower than when you go for a walk with Tom, and he has to collect up every stone. Because Beatrice stopped every few steps. And sometimes she tried to sit down. And at the bottom of the road she went solid, like a statue, and refused to turn right, so we had to go left instead. And Suzanne pulled at the *front* end of Beatrice, and I pushed at the *back* end, all the way down the hill, and into the village. It wasn't much fun, not like when we used to go with Barney, and you had to run to keep up, and he sniffed every lamp post, and barked at cars, and people waved, or gave him a pat, and said, "Looks like the dog's taking *you* for a walk" and things like that. Because no one said anything about Beatrice. Except a man at the bottom bus stop, who shook his head, and said, "Tut, tut, tut, shame."

When we got to the bridge, Beatrice went solid like a statue, again, just like she had at the bottom of our road, and we couldn't get her to go over.

"Let's turn around and go home," I said.

Suzanne pulled and I pushed. But Beatrice wouldn't turn around.

"She doesn't *want* to go home," Suzanne said. "I told you she'd like it once she got going. We'll have to turn right, and go along the river."

I didn't want to go along the river because for one thing it was cold, and for another thing it was getting dark, and for an even other thing, I don't like the ducks.

"Unless you're scared of the *ducks*?" Suzanne asked.

"No," I said. Because I'm not scared of *most* ducks. Because most ducks just bob along on the water, and waddle about, and wait for bits of bread. But the ducks down by the river are different. Because there are millions of them. They live on the island in the middle. And they go around in gangs. And there's one that's the leader, which is bigger, with an extra long neck, and a white eye that looks off in the wrong direction. And Graham Roberts said it got crossed with a *swan*. And it could break your arm. Which is probably true. Because Graham lives on a farm.

"The ducks won't bother us when they see Beatrice," Suzanne said. "I'll let her off the lead and she can charge, like Barney used to, and send them all scattering."

We started down the path that leads to the riverbank. When we got to the bit where the grass opens out, Suzanne unclipped Beatrice's lead. "You're off the lead, Beatrice." She patted her side, "You're *free!*"

Beatrice stood still.

"*Run*, Beatrice!"

Beatrice started walking slowly forwards.

"Maybe if we ran around ourselves," said Suzanne, "that might get Beatrice going." So me and Suzanne chased each other, and jumped up and down, and clapped our hands. And threw sticks, and said, "*Come on*, Beatrice" and "Good dog" and "Off you go!" And we ran ahead, past the bin, and the gorse bushes, and up to the bench where the old people always sit.

And then we sat down and waited for Beatrice to catch up. And we walked on, to the row of cottages whose gardens go down to the riverbank.

When we came to the last cottage, Beatrice stopped. And sat down in front of it. The gate to the cottage was covered in ivy. There was a 'for sale' sign next to it. Beatrice pushed at the gate with her nose.

"What's she *doing*?" I asked.

Beatrice rubbed her head against the gate, and whimpered.

"She wants to go *in*." Suzanne said. We leant on the gate and looked over. There was a big kennel at the top of the garden. Suzanne looked at the kennel. And then she looked at the gate. And she pulled some of the ivy away from the nameplate. And she read it. "Sorrel Cottage. It says *Sorrel Cottage*, Anna."

"So?"

"So…" Suzanne said, "look at what it says on the *kennel*…"

Above the arch of the door, there was a name. "It says *Beatrice*!"

"This is Aunt *Deidra's* house, where Beatrice *lived*."

Beatrice put her nose in the air, and made a strange howling noise. Like the whale music that Mrs Peters puts on in P.E. for Free Movement.

Suzanne tried the gate. It was locked.

"Let's go home," I said. Because it was cold and was starting to get dark and the ducks were probably coming.

Suzanne held her finger up, and looked Beatrice in the eye, and started talking in her special dog-training voice, again, "*Beatrice, come...*" Beatrice didn't budge. Suzanne clipped the lead onto Beatrice's collar and gave it a little tug. Then she gave it a bigger tug. Then she put it over her shoulder, and pulled as hard as she could, "Uungh...."

"Try giving her one of the S.N.A.C.K.S," I said. Because when Suzanne had Barney, she could make him do anything for a snack, especially for one of Carl's rice-cakes.

"You're only supposed to give S.N.A.C.K.S for *good* behaviour," Suzanne said. But she got the packet out of her pocket. Beatrice looked at them. Then she looked back at the gate and made the whale noises louder than ever. And

then I heard *another* noise, nearby.

"**Quack**."

"What was that?"

"What?"

"I heard something."

"**Quack**."

"Over there"

"**Quack**."

I turned around.

"**Quack**, **Quack**."

Three ducks waddled out of the water and up the bank towards us.

"Ducks," Suzanne said. "Ducks, Beatrice, *charge!*" But Beatrice didn't even turn around.

I clapped my hands at them. "Shoo." The ducks stopped.

Then, "**Quack**."

"On your left, Anna." Four more ducks came waddling out from in the gorse bushes. I turned around and ran at them, and waved my arms.

"**Quack**." Four more ducks appeared on the right, from in the long grass.

"Let's *go*," I said, "before they get us *surrounded*."

Suzanne pulled at Beatrice's lead. "I'll get Beatrice up, Anna. You fend off the ducks." Suzanne got a rice cake out of the packet and held it up in front of Beatrice. The ducks started flapping their wings, and quacking like mad, and waddling forwards together.

Then, "**HONK**." The Swan Duck with the long neck, and the white eye that looks off the wrong way, shoved its way to the front. It stuck

its neck forward, with its head on the side. And its good eye looked at Beatrice, and Suzanne, and the snacks. And the white eye, which looks off the wrong way, was watching *me*. "**HONK!**"

Suzanne jumped. Some of the rice cakes went up in the air, and fell on the ground around Beatrice. The Swan Duck stuck out its chest, and reared up, and opened its wings. It hissed, "**TSSSSS!**" And rushed forward. And the other ducks came behind it. All flapping and pecking and quacking like mad. At the ricecakes, and the ground, and Beatrice.

Beatrice put her nose further in the air and made the whale noises louder than ever.

"DO SOMETHING, SUZANNE!"

Suzanne threw the bag of rice cakes as far as she could. The ducks ran after them, the

Swan Duck first, all quacking and flapping and pecking at the snacks and each other. Suzanne grabbed the end of Beatrice's lead, and pulled as hard as she could. I got down on the ground, and wriggled my shoulder right under Beatrice. "Three, two, one..." I closed my eyes, and pushed forward and up. Beatrice's back end wobbled a bit. *"Nngnngya!"*

Beatrice was on her feet. And we set off up over the fields, so we didn't have to go back past the ducks, and turned right onto the road that leads back into the village, pushing and pulling Beatrice, and stopping and starting, all the way home.

CHAPTER 9
"That Damn Dog!"

Me and Suzanne took Beatrice for another walk the next morning, before school. And when we got back from school, we took her out again. And the next day we did the same, and the day after that. And Suzanne said how when Beatrice was settled in, she would walk faster, and wag her tail, and she wouldn't always only go left at the bottom of the road, and right at the river, and stop outside Sorrel Cottage to make whale noises. Because Suzanne was going to start training Beatrice, and soon she would be fetching sticks, and doing tricks, and charging at the ducks and sending them all scattering, like Barney used to. And we could do races with her up the road, and go out on our bikes, and set up obstacle courses and all that. Instead of levering her up, and pulling and pushing and stopping and starting, and defending her from ducks, and picking up her poos in the garage when we got back.

But when the weekend came, Beatrice was still the same, and then another week went past, and she still wasn't better. And, if anything, she'd got worse. Because she was walking round and round in circles, in the garage, and refusing to eat her food, and making whale noises all night. Until one night Suzanne's Dad pulled his earplugs out and said,

"SOMETHING HAS TO BE DONE ABOUT THAT DAMN DOG!"

So Suzanne's Mum made an appointment for Beatrice at the Vet's.

The Vet looked with a little torch in Beatrice's ears, and her eyes. And she checked all the way down her back, and felt up and down her legs and lifted up each paw. And she listened to Beatrice's heart. And she looked serious and said, "*Hmmm…*" and "Oh *dear*", and "*That's* not good." And when she was finished, she said, "Beatrice has a few issues, I'm afraid. Starting at the top and working our way down…"

She pointed to different bits of Beatrice. "She has a septic wound on the top of her head; numerous small tumours above her eyes; a nasty nasal infection, leading to secondary inflammation in the ear, just here, behind this build-up of wax; abscesses on two teeth; serious cavities in three; general build-up of tartar and, judging by her breath, some kind of serious gastric problem. Moving down, possible arthritis of the spine, and almost certainly in the hips; limber tail syndrome; worms, I suspect; some rather inflamed flea-bites…"

A pool of water appeared on the floor, between Beatrice's back legs.

"Oh, and she's incontinent."

This is what it says incontinence is in my dictionary…

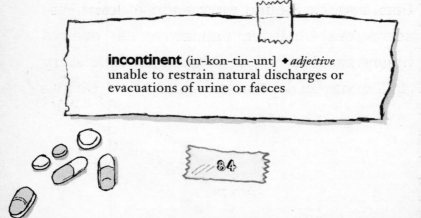

incontinent (in-kon-tin-unt) ◆ *adjective*
unable to restrain natural discharges or evacuations of urine or faeces

"I can treat some of the more minor issues now, while you wait: lancing the abscess, putting a couple of stitches in, addressing the ear wax build-up, an injection of antibiotics for the nasal infection, and a worming pill. The rest will require further investigation, longer appointments, and of course, with her age, you'll want to consider the *cost*."

The Vet pulled a pair of rubber gloves on. "The pointed scalpel, please, Patricia." And put a white mask over her mouth. "It's probably best if you wait outside."

Me and Suzanne and Suzanne's Mum went back into the waiting room and sat down. We could hear Beatrice making whale noises behind the door.

"Do you think Beatrice is alright?"

"She will be," Suzanne said, "once the Vet has finished, won't she, Mum?"

"Beatrice has lots of things wrong with her, Suzanne."

"Yes, but once the Vet's fixed them, she'll be fine."

After ages, the nurse brought Beatrice out into the waiting room. She had a bandage on her left front leg, a shaved patch on her back, and a white plastic cone around her head. She looked worse than ever.

Suzanne's Mum went to the

reception desk.

"This is the bill for today's procedures," the Nurse said.

Suzanne's Mum looked at it. Her eyebrows went up.

"And these, here, are some of the more complicated treatments that Beatrice needs, along with the estimated costs."

Suzanne's Mum's eyebrows went up even higher. "How long does she have to keep the cone on for?"

"At least a week," the nurse said, "to stop her scratching her stitches."

Suzanne took Beatrice's lead from the nurse.

"Come, Beatrice." She gave the lead a little tug. Then she gave it a bigger tug. Then she

put it over her shoulder and pulled as hard as she could, "Uungh . . ." Beatrice stood still.

I got down on the ground, and wriggled my shoulder right under Beatrice, and held my breath.

"Three, two, one… *Lift-off.*"

I pushed forward and up as hard as I could. Beatrice's back end wobbled a bit.

"That's it, Anna, *push.*"

"Nngnngya!"

ꞏ CHAPTER 10 ꞏ
A Dog's Life

This is a list of all the things I do on school days since Suzanne got Beatrice.

6.00:   Alarm goes off. Press snooze.

6.05:   Alarm goes off. Press snooze.

6.10:   Alarm goes off. Mum comes in: "Anna, stop pressing snooze and turn off that alarm!" Turn off alarm. Get out of bed. Put coat and wellies on over pyjamas. Meet Suzanne out the front.

6.15: Lever Beatrice up and push her all the way to the river.

7.00: Wait while Beatrice makes whale noises at Great Aunt Deidra's gate. Defend Beatrice from ducks. Throw rice cakes to keep ducks busy.

7.30: Lever Beatrice up while ducks eat rice cakes and attack each other. Push Beatrice all the way home.

8.15: Pick up Beatrice's poos in Suzanne's garage.

8.30: Wash dead vole smell off in shower. Eat cornflakes.

8.45: Go to school. Try not to fall asleep at desk.

90

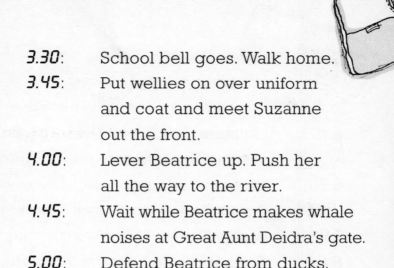

3.30: School bell goes. Walk home.

3.45: Put wellies on over uniform and coat and meet Suzanne out the front.

4.00: Lever Beatrice up. Push her all the way to the river.

4.45: Wait while Beatrice makes whale noises at Great Aunt Deidra's gate.

5.00: Defend Beatrice from ducks. Throw rice cakes to keep ducks busy.

5.15: Lever Beatrice up while ducks eat rice cakes and attack each other. Push Beatrice all the way back home.

6.00: Pick up poos in Suzanne's garage.

91

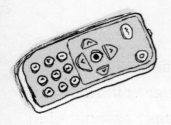

6.15: Go home and wash dead vole smell off in shower.

6.30: Eat tea. Wash up.

7.00: Do homework.

7.45: Watch telly.

8.00: Go to bed.

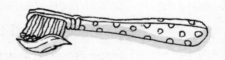

And weekends weren't much better. Because as well as taking Beatrice for two walks a day, there were other jobs to do for her, like sweeping up all her hair in the garage, and mopping the floor with disinfectant because of all the wees and poos in the week, and washing her bedding, and going shopping for dog food. And I was getting sick of doing things for Beatrice because it was better before, when me and Suzanne could do other stuff on Saturdays, like throwing the practice rope from Lifesavers to each other in the back lane, and going in the shed, and making up passwords, and plans, and doing spy clubs and all that.

So that Saturday I asked Suzanne, "Do we *have* to take Beatrice for a walk today?"

"Yes."

"Why?"

"Because walks are on the list we made of Reasons to Get Great Aunt Deidra's Dog."

"What about if we just took her for *one*

walk, then?"

"The list says 'two' and it's underlined. And it's on the fridge. Where Dad can see it. And if I miss anything he can send Beatrice back to Aunt Deidra's Nephew, Mick."

Suzanne clipped Beatrice's lead onto her collar. "Come."

Beatrice didn't come.

"Heel." Beatrice didn't budge.

"You'll have to lever her up, Anna."

"Maybe *you* could be in charge of the back end of Beatrice today, and lever her up, and hold the nappy bags and all that. And pick up the poos in the garage after, and I'll be in charge of the *front* for once?"

But Suzanne said how Beatrice would get confused, and it might set her back in her training and all that.

So I got down on the ground and wriggled my shoulder right under Beatrice, and tried not to think about where my nose was. Which was hard, with the dead vole smell and all that.

And we walked down to the river, pushing and pulling Beatrice, and stopping and starting. And we waited while Beatrice made whale noises. And we defended her from the ducks. And threw the rice cakes to distract them. And I got underneath Beatrice again, and levered her back up. And we went home over the fields. Pushing and pulling Beatrice, and stopping and starting. And into Suzanne's garage. And Suzanne tipped the old food and water out, and put new in. And I picked up Beatrice's poos, and put them in nappy bags. And then we swept the floor to get all the hairs up, and mopped it with disinfectant. And Beatrice sat in the back lane, between the bins.

"Can we *please* go in the shed now, and make up a password, and put the lock on, and do some plans and all that?" I asked.

"I need to train Beatrice to fetch a stick first," Suzanne said, and she went out into the back lane.

"Beatrice *can't* fetch," I said.

"She can," Suzanne said, "she just doesn't know what 'fetch' means yet. I have to keep on training her so she doesn't forget the parts of the trick she's already learned."

"She hasn't learned *any* parts of it," I said. Which was

96

true. Because there's only two parts to fetching a stick, the getting it part, and the bringing it back part, and Beatrice had never done either of them.

Suzanne looked the other way, like she always does when she doesn't like what you say, and she threw the stick anyway. "Fetch."

Beatrice stayed where she was.

"Fetch." Suzanne pointed to the stick.

"Fetch the stick, Beatrice."

Beatrice yawned.

"Maybe if *you* went and got the stick, Anna, and brought it back, that would show Beatrice what fetching *is*."

So I ran down the lane and got the stick and brought it back to Suzanne.

"Beatrice is definitely watching you," Suzanne

said. She threw the stick again. "Fetch!" And again. "Try running a bit faster, Anna." And after about a million times of Suzanne telling me to 'fetch', I stopped and said, "No." Because for one thing it's not much fun fetching a stick, and that's probably why Beatrice didn't want to do it. And for another thing, Beatrice wasn't watching, because her eyes were closed, and she had fallen asleep.

"Let's go in the shed."

"Only if Beatrice can come with us," Suzanne said.

"Beatrice is too big to fit."

"We could take out the deck-chairs and the bikes and deflate the dinghy."

"It's only supposed to be me and you allowed in the shed."

"Tom sometimes comes in."

"That's different."

"How?"

"Because Tom's smaller than Beatrice," I said, "and he doesn't wee on the floor."

"Yes he does."

"Only once," I said. And it didn't count because it was hide-and-seek, and he had been there for ages, and he didn't want to come out, in case Suzanne saw him.

"Well, it does count, actually," Suzanne said, "because it still smells in that corner."

"No it doesn't."

"It does. It *stinks*."

"Not as much as Beatrice."

"Beatrice doesn't stink."

"She does," I said, "because her front end stinks like Mrs Constantine's pond, the time it went slimy and the fish floated to the top, and her back end stinks like Graham Roberts' dead vole. And she probably stinks in the *middle* as well."

And Suzanne went quiet and didn't say anything. And then she said that Beatrice didn't *want* to go in the shed and do Shed Club anyway, and neither did *she*. And she was going to set up her *own* club, in the garage, called Garage Club, which only her and Beatrice were allowed in.

And I said, "Good." And I went to the shed by myself and I put the lock on the door and made up a password, which was, 'I Hate Beatrice.'

CHAPTER 11
Spy Club

After Suzanne left Shed Club and started up Garage Club with Beatrice, I got all of Suzanne's things off the shelf, like the piccalilli jar with her adenoids in, and her Dad's French-English, English-French dictionary and I put them outside in the lane. And then I took her name off the 'Keep Out! By Order of Anna and Suzanne' sign on the shed door. So it just said, 'Keep Out! By Order of Anna.' And off 'Anna's and Suzanne's Club Rules And Regulations.' And off the Spy Club Notebook.

And I opened the notebook up and I flicked past the pages for all the people that me and Suzanne had spied on, 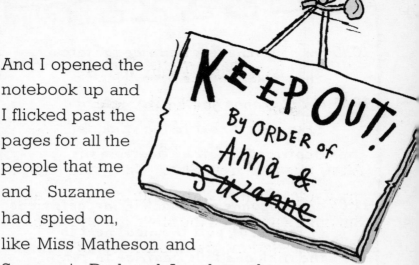 like Miss Matheson and Suzanne's Dad and Joe-down-the-road's Mum's Old Boyfriend. And I got the binoculars Mrs Rotherham gave us down off the shelf, and looked through the spy hole. And I started a new page in the Spy Club Notebook. And I put, 'Suzanne and Beatrice' at the top.

10.45 am – Suzanne tells Beatrice to "fetch" the stick. Beatrice sits by bins.

10.51 am – Suzanne goes inside, gets rice cake, puts it next to the stick, tells Beatrice to "fetch". Beatrice sits by bins.

11.03 am – Suzanne goes back inside, gets piece of raw meat, puts the meat next to the stick and tells Beatrice to "Fetch". Beatrice sits by bins.

11.27 am – Suzanne breaks the meat up into little pieces to make a trail, going all the way from Beatrice to the stick, and tells Beatrice to "fetch". Beatrice sits by bins. Suzanne breaks the stick then shouts, "OH WHY WON'T YOU JUST FETCH THE STICK, LIKE BARNEY USED TO, BEATRICE!"

> 11.28 am – Suzanne's Dad comes out, sees the trail of meat and goes mad, "THAT'S A TEN POUND PIECE OF PRIME FILLET, FOR CRYING OUT LOUD!" Suzanne's Dad goes back inside. Suzanne sits by Beatrice, by the bins.

After a while I got sick of Spy Club, because it's better when there's two of you doing it, like when it's me and Suzanne, and we take it in turns to look through the binoculars. And one of us says what's happening, and the other one checks the times, and writes it all down. So I went to find Tom.

Tom was out the front, with Mr Tucker. "Ah ha, Popsie, come to help me and Basher check the old weather measuring apparatus, eh?"

"No," I said. Because I hadn't. "I've come to ask Tom something."

"Fire away."

"It's *secret*."

Mr Tucker covered his ears.

"Do you want to come and do Spy Club?" I whispered. And I put my hand in front of my mouth because Mr Tucker didn't look like he was covering his ears properly, and he was in the war and all that, and he probably knows how to lip-read.

"Who are you spying on?" Tom asked.

"Suzanne," I said, "and Beatrice."

"No thanks," Tom said. "Beatrice is too big. Me and Mr Tucker are spotting clouds."

"What do you say, Popsie? We could do with another pair of eyes. See that one, shaped like a dog? That's a cirrus. Perfectly harmless more often than not but *could* indicate an approaching storm…"

"No thanks," I said. Because I didn't want to spot clouds.

I went inside to see Mum. Mum was getting dirty washing out of the basket. "There's no one to do clubs with."

"Where's Suzanne?"

"We're not friends. She's in her own Club, with Beatrice."

"You can be in my club if you like."

"What's it called?"

"Washing Club. We sort the washing into three piles. Whites, darks, and lights, and take the *biggest* pile to the *machine* and..."

I turned round. "No. I don't want to be in Washing Club."

Because it didn't sound very good.

Mum called after me, "Neither do *I*."

And I went up the road to see Mrs Rotherham instead

Mrs Rotherham put the kettle on and made some tea and brought out the biscuits. I told her how Suzanne had left Shed Club. And started up Garage Club, with Beatrice. And how we weren't friends anymore. Because all Suzanne wanted to do was train Beatrice to fetch a stick, and take her for walks, instead of going in the shed and doing plans and clubs and all that. And how I always had to be in charge of the back end of Beatrice, and lever her up and pick up the poos. And how Beatrice was the worst dog anyone ever had, because she never wagged her tail, or jumped up, or ran, and she hardly ate any food, and she weed everywhere all the time, even in her own bed, and pooed in the garage, and walked round in circles and made whale noises all night.

And Mrs Rotherham listened, and said, "Well, well, well", and "I see", and "Oh dear, oh dear, oh dear."

And she told me about how when she was in the police they had a police dog, called Colin, who had a handler called Stan. And

Colin and Stan did everything together. And when Stan retired, Colin sat in Stan's parking space, for a week, and whined. And the Vet said Colin was depressed, which meant he was sad all the time. "It sounds to me like Beatrice might be depressed as well," Mrs Rotherham said.

And I said how Beatrice probably *was*. Because I would be sad all the time if *I* was Beatrice. Especially if I had to be in Garage Club with Suzanne and she kept trying to make me get a stick.

When I got back to the shed I looked depression up in my dictionary. This is what it said:

depression [di-presh-un] ◆ *noun*
a condition of general emotional dejection and withdrawal; sadness greater and more prolonged than that warranted by any objective reason

And then I went on the computer and I put 'depressed dog' in. And I found a page all about what makes dogs depressed. And it said the top three things were…

1. A change in environment, such as moving house.
2. A bereavement: the loss of a good doggie or human friend.
3. Physical problems: aches, pains, or illness.

And *Beatrice* had moved house, *and* she had lost Aunt Deidra, and she *definitely* had aches and pains and illnesses because she still hadn't been back to the Vet's.

And there was a 'Is Your Dog Depressed?' questionnaire, to find out whether or not your dog has got it. And 'Advice On Helping A Depressed Dog' as well. So I went and got the printer cable from on top of the kitchen cupboard, which is where Mum hides it to stop me printing things off which she says I don't need, like two hundred and forty three pages for Tom about Batman and Bob the Builder. And I printed off all the pages about dogs and being depressed.

And then I went out to the shed, and I got all Suzanne's things which I'd put outside, in the lane, like her piccalilli jar and her French-English, English-French Dictionary, and I put them back in the shed, on the shelf. And I wrote Suzanne's name back on the 'Keep Out!

By Order of Anna' sign on the shed door, so it said 'Anna and Suzanne' again. And on the Club Rules and Regulations. And in the Spy Club Notebook. And I got a piece of paper, and a pen, and I put:

You are hereby invited to join

Shed Club
VID

(which means 'Very Important Dog')

Lifelong Membership

You are bound by the rules and regulations of Shed Club, available on request.

And I put the invitation in an envelope. And wrote 'Beatrice' on the front of it. And went round to Suzanne's. And I rang the bell three times, because me and Suzanne always do things in threes if it's something important, and I posted the invitation through the Barrys' letterbox. And then I ran away because it was Saturday and Suzanne's Dad was home, and he was already annoyed about his piece of prime fillet.

I went back to the shed, and waited.

And after ages I saw Suzanne, through the spyhole, coming up the back-lane, moving Beatrice's feet forward, one at a time.

So I went and pushed the back end of Beatrice. And Suzanne pulled the front. And we didn't say anything. And we took the bikes out of the shed, and the deck-chairs, and the dinghy, to make more room inside. And we both got underneath Beatrice, to lever her up into the shed.

"There," Suzanne said. "She does fit."

"Yes. And she doesn't stink." Which wasn't exactly true, especially once the door was closed. Because it's very small inside the shed. And it was quite hard to breathe.

Suzanne got two dust masks down off one of the shelves in the shed, which Dad uses when he's decorating.

"Gas masks," she said. And we put them on. And closed the door again. And it still smelt pretty bad, because even though the masks can stop dust, they couldn't block out Beatrice. Suzanne got some blu-tack

↑ blu-tack

down off the shelf. She pulled two bits off and rolled them into balls, and put one in each nostril. And I did the same. And we put the gas masks back on again. Which was much better. And I told Suzanne all about what Mrs Rotherham said about Colin the police dog, and Stan, and how Colin got depressed when Stan left. And I had to say it quite loud and clear because the blu-tack made me sound bunged up, and the dust mask muffled my mouth, and because Beatrice had started snoring.

I showed Suzanne the 'Is Your Dog Depressed?' questionnaire. And Suzanne said I should read out the questions. And she would answer them. So that's what we did.

"Does your dog look sad and mopey?"

"Yes."

"Does your dog sleep most of the time?"

"Yes."

"Does your dog have no interest in toys or games?"

"Yes."

"Does your dog have a poor appetite?"

"Yes."

"Does your dog prefer to be alone?"

"Yes."

"If you have ticked 'yes' for three or more of the above questions, your dog is depressed."

Suzanne counted the ticks, "Five. That's all of them." And we read the page called Advice On Helping A Depressed Dog, and Suzanne said we should make a list of all the things it said we could do to help Beatrice get better.

So we did.

ANNA'S AND SUZANNE'S LIST OF THINGS TO DO TO HELP STOP BEATRICE BEING DEPRESSED

1. Increase your dog's self esteem by frequent shows of affection (both verbal and physical). Encourage friends and family to do the same.
2. Make arrangements so that your dog is not left alone.
3. Take your dog to places that will lift its spirit.
4. Get another dog to keep your depressed dog company.
5. Have your dog assessed by a Vet and carry out any recommended treatments.

CHAPTER 12
Making Beatrice Better

The first thing on the list was to give Beatrice verbal and physical affection. This is what it says about 'verbal' in my dictionary...

verbal [vur-bul] ◆ *adjective*
consisting of or expressed in words
(as opposed to actions): eg. a verbal protest

And this is what it says physical is...

physical (fizz-i-cul) ◆ *adjective*
Pertaining to or connected with the body

We did the verbal affection first, and told Beatrice what a good dog she was, and said how nice it was to see her, and told her how lovely she looked (which wasn't exactly true because she still had the cone on, and the bald patch, and the bandage and all that). And then it was time for the physical affection. It wasn't easy to give Beatrice physical affection, because of the vole smell at the back and the fish pond smell at the front. So we decided before we gave Beatrice physical affection we better give her a bath. So Suzanne went into her house, and I went into mine. And Suzanne brought out Carl's baby bath, and some shampoo and conditioner and her Mum's hairdressing kit. And I got a towel and Dad's face flannel, and a pair of washing-up

120

gloves and Mum's perfume. And we took the cone off Beatrice's neck, carefully, and the bandage from her front leg. And we attached the hose to the tap in Suzanne's kitchen, and made sure the water came through nice and warm, and not too fast, and we filled up Carl's baby bath, and lifted up Beatrice's front paws, one at a time, and put them in it. And as soon as she felt her paws in the water, Beatrice's tail came out from between her legs, and she stopped staring at the floor, and looked up. And she moved her front paws up and down in the baby bath, and put her whole head in the water and moved it from side to side.

"She *loves* it," Suzanne said.

Me and Suzanne picked the

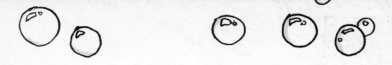

baby bath up, and tipped it over Beatrice. And Beatrice wagged her tail like mad, and then she lay down in the water, in the lane, and rolled over and over. And I ran in and turned the hose on again, and Suzanne held it over Beatrice. And we shampooed her head, and all down her back, and each side. And I did her face with Dad's flannel, and got the sleep out of her eyes. And I put the washing-up gloves on to do the matted bits round her bum. And we went down each leg to her paws and right to the tip of her tail. And then we rinsed it off, and shampooed her again, because it said on the bottle "repeat if necessary." And it was necessary with Beatrice. Because the water that was running off into the gutter was black.

And then we put conditioner on, and combed it through, and massaged the ends. And let it soak in for deep conditioning, like it said. And Beatrice stood very still, and half closed her eyes, and put her nose up in the air. And Suzanne said how when they had Barney, he hated being bathed. And he would never just stand still and let you do it, like Beatrice, because they had to hold him down.

And then we rinsed the conditioner off, and dried Beatrice with the towel. And she shook herself. And we got Suzanne's Mum's hair-dryer, and plugged it in in the garage, and put the diffuser attachment on, for curly hair, and dried her with that. And Suzanne trimmed Beatrice's fringe with her Mum's hairdressing scissors. And I did two squirts of Mum's

123

perfume on Beatrice's bum.

And then me and Suzanne stood back, to have a proper look at Beatrice. And she looked a lot better. And she smelt a lot better too, especially at the back, because we did a sniff test. And we couldn't smell dead vole. But she still smelt like Mrs Constantine's green pond when the fish died at the front.

"We better brush Beatrice's teeth," Suzanne said.

Suzanne ran into her house and got some toothpaste, and I ran into mine and got the old toothbrush Mum keeps under the sink for cleaning between the tiles. And we put the blu-tack back in our noses, and put the dust masks on, and I put the rubber gloves on, and held Beatrice's mouth open, which Beatrice didn't mind. And Suzanne brushed Beatrice's teeth. And it took quite a long time, and a *lot* of toothpaste, because Beatrice had lots of teeth and they were very big and very dirty.

And Suzanne did the sniff test again. She shook her head. "We need something stronger."

So I went into my house and I got mouthwash. And Suzanne went into her house and got her Dad's electric toothbrush. And she switched it to 'powerful' and brushed Beatrice's teeth again. And then we flossed in-between them. And put some of the mouthwash in Beatrice's water bowl for her to rinse. And we both did the sniff test again, together, and we could

still smell Mrs Constantine's pond a bit, so Suzanne went inside and got a pack of extra strong mints. And she put one into Beatrice's mouth. And she put her arms around Beatrice's neck, and rested her cheek against Beatrice's, and gave her a squeeze. And Beatrice closed her eyes, and moved her head up and down against Suzanne, like she does with Great Aunt Deidra's gate. And I stroked Beatrice's back, and her chest, and her fur felt all warm and soft, and I rubbed behind her ears. And then we went to take Beatrice to see some family and friends, to get affection off them, because that's what it said on the list.

"What's that dog doing in here?" Mum said.

"Beatrice is depressed," I said. "You have to say something nice."

"You smell better, Beatrice. Is that my *perfume*, Anna?"

"No. And now you have to stroke her."

Mum patted Beatrice on the head, and stroked her behind the ears. "Poor old Beatrice. There. Now get her out please, Anna, before she pees all over the...oh, no, *Beatrice*..."

Tom came into the kitchen. "What's that?"

"Wee," Mum said. She got some kitchen roll and started cleaning it up.

"Beatrice is sad," I said.

"Does she need a biscuit?"

"No," Mum said, "she doesn't need a biscuit. Don't stand *there*, Tom, you'll get your feet in it. What she *needs* is a nappy."

"That's it...!" Suzanne ran home.

"You're only supposed to say nice things to

127

Beatrice," I said. "Now you've upset Suzanne."

But Suzanne wasn't upset. Because she came straight back. With a packet of Carl's nappies. She pulled one out. "Locks in leaks for up to twelve hours of protection."

"It's a bit small," I said. "How are we going to attach it on?"

"We could put it inside some big pants, and put the pants on Beatrice?"

"No one wears pants big enough to fit Beatrice," Mum said.

"What about bears?" Tom said.

"Or Mrs Rotherham?" I said. Because her pants are enormous. Even bigger than Nanna's pants used to be. I've seen them hanging on the line.

"You are *not* to go and ask Mrs Rotherham for pants," Mum said.

"Come on, Beatrice." Suzanne pulled the lead. Beatrice didn't budge. I got down underneath her and levered her up.

"Anna, did you hear me?"

But we were already outside.

Suzanne explained to Mrs Rotherham about how Beatrice was depressed. And how we had made a list of things to do to help her get better. And how it was hard to get people to give her affection when she was weeing all over their kitchen floor.

And Mrs Rotherham said, "I quite understand," and she put some newspaper down, and she asked us in.

And Suzanne showed Mrs Rotherham Carl's nappy and said how we didn't know how to attach it on.

"If only we had some really big pants…" I said.

Mrs Rotherham looked at Beatrice. And she looked at me and Suzanne. And she winked. And she went into her cupboard, and she brought out a packet with some pants in, and she passed it to Suzanne.

Suzanne read the back: "High-waisted, low-legged hosiery with controlling compression zones for security and confidence. Large." Suzanne took a pair out of the pack and held them up against Beatrice. "They're too small."

Mrs Rotherham got out some scissors, and she cut right down each leg of both of the pairs of pants, and went over to her sewing machine, and sewed the two pairs together to make an even bigger pair, and she cut out a hole for Beatrice's tail.

Suzanne lifted up Beatrice's back paws, and put them into the legs of the pants, and we started pulling them up. Which was quite hard because of the 'controlling compression zones'.

Mrs Rotherham started getting The Hysterics when she saw Beatrice in the pants. And me and Suzanne got The Hysterics as well. But not as much as Mrs Rotherham. Because she had to lean against the wall, and get her breath back. And then Suzanne said we should stop laughing because it wasn't very nice for Beatrice.

And Mrs Rotherham said, "Quite right."

Suzanne pulled Beatrice's tail through the hole and put the nappy in, underneath.

And Mrs Rotherham got us some ice cream because, like Nanna used to say, ice cream is good when you need to calm down. And she got a bowl of water for Beatrice. And Beatrice lay down, and fell asleep on the black sheepskin rug, in front of Mrs Rotherham's fire. And Mrs Rotherham sat in her chair, next to Beatrice, and stroked Beatrice's ears, while me and Suzanne ate our ice cream. And you could hardly tell Beatrice was there, apart from the cone and the bandage, and the pants, because she blended right into the rug.

Me and Suzanne showed Mrs Rotherham the list of things we were going to do to make Beatrice better. And Mrs Rotherham said she could help us with Number 2, because we could take Beatrice round to her house in the mornings, if we liked, before school, so Beatrice wouldn't have to stay in the garage on her own all day.

And we said thank you to Mrs Rotherham, and we took Beatrice to get affection off other friends and family, like Mr Tucker, and Joe-down-the-road, and Joe-down-the-road's Mum, like it said on the list. And they were all pleased to see Beatrice, and her pants. And

Suzanne said she thought the pants *had* given Beatrice security and confidence, like it said on the pack. Because her head wasn't down, looking at the ground anymore. And we went back to the shed, and ticked off Number 1 on the list, and Number 2 as well, which was "Make arrangements so that your dog is not left alone".

Number 3 was to take Beatrice to places to lift her spirit. And the next day was Sunday, so Suzanne said that, in the morning, after we had taken Beatrice for her walk, we should take her to church, because that's where they talk about lifting spirits, and all that.

CHAPTER 13
The Ark

When she saw Beatrice, Mrs Constantine said, "No, definitely not, no pets, I'm afraid." Mrs Constantine is the Vicar's wife. She is in charge of Sunday School.

"If I allow one, I'll have to allow everyone. Next thing, Graham Roberts will have his ferret in the font again."

Suzanne told Mrs Constantine about Beatrice being depressed, and how she wasn't supposed to be left on her own, and how we had brought her to church to have her Spirit Uplifted. And she showed her the list of things to help Beatrice get better.

"I see. Why is she wearing pants?"

"To keep her nappy in place."

"Mmm."

Mrs Constantine didn't look very pleased, "You can bring her in just this once. Keep her away from the model ark, please. The Vicar wants it on the trestle table in the north transept before communion starts."

We had been working on the ark at Sunday School for three weeks. It was papier mâché and painted in all bright colours with a ramp for the animals to walk up and there was a piece of blue satin to put underneath it for the flood waters. And we had each made a pair of animals, out of coloured paper, and pasta shapes, and bits from the fabric box, and all that, to put in it. Apart from Emma Hendry, because she had

made Noah and his wife. And Graham Roberts, because he had made cages. Mrs Constantine didn't want cages in the ark, because she said she didn't think cages would be very pretty. But Graham made them anyway because he said, "It won't be pretty if we *don't* have cages. It'll be a *bloodbath*."

Anyway, Emma Hendry put Noah and his wife in, and Joe-down-the-road put his rabbits in, and Tom put in his slugs (which were meant to be cats at first but Tom made them out of a toilet roll's inside, and tissue paper, and he poured the glue on, instead of using the spatula, and they collapsed). And then Shelly Wainwright put her sheep in, and Suzanne went to put her dogs down, next to Shelly's sheep.

"Are those sheepdogs?" Graham Roberts asked.

"No, they're terriers."

"You can't put terriers there," Graham said. "They'll worry the sheep. They'll have to have a cage."

Suzanne stuck the dogs down. "Yes, you

can. My dog Barney's a terrier and when he stopped living with us my Dad took him to *live* on a farm. He roams free, in the fields, and he's better off."

"If a farmer sees a dog in with his sheep, he's allowed to shoot it." Graham lives on a farm. With his Gran.

"Farmers aren't allowed to shoot dogs."

"Yes they are. My Grandad told me." Graham's Grandad was a farmer. Before he died. "He once had to shoot a dog himself."

"That's a lie," Suzanne said. And Graham got cross and said it wasn't a lie because his Grandad didn't tell lies. It was Suzanne's Dad who was a liar. Because he probably said her dog was roaming free on a farm so he didn't have to tell her it was dead.

"Barney isn't dead!" Suzanne *pushed* Graham Roberts. And Graham Roberts fell over.

And then he got up, and he pushed Suzanne back. "Yes he is. And your Dad probably had him put down." And Suzanne fell onto Beatrice. And Beatrice fell onto the ark.

And Emma Hendry shouted, "Bad Dog!" And Beatrice started making her whale noises. And Shelly Wainwright started shouting about her sheep. Me and Suzanne levered Beatrice up. The ark was squashed flat. And so were all the animals. And it was wet as well. Because Beatrice's nappy leaked.

"This is *exactly* why I said No Pets in the *first* place!" Mrs Constantine told us to take Beatrice home.

Me and Tom and Suzanne and Beatrice went outside. The sky had gone dark, like at night.

"It's the dog cloud," Tom said. "Look." He pointed at the storm cloud he and Mr Tucker had spotted before. We passed the side door of the church, which was open, and we could hear the Vicar inside: "And God looked upon the earth, and God said unto Noah, the earth is filled with *violence* and behold I do bring a *flood of waters* . . . ."

CHAPTER 14
Misty

When we got into our road Mr Tucker was in his front garden, tying up Mrs Tucker's plants. Tom showed him his slugs, and told him all about the ark and how it got squashed. And how he was going to have to get his *own* ark now, to put his slugs in, for when the flood started, and he was going to use the dinghy from the shed.

"Good plan, Basher. Look at those cirrus there. And a sudden fall on the barometer too this morning. Doesn't bode well for Mrs Tucker's honeysuckle. Hope there's space in the ark for an Old Lag like myself." And Tom said that there was. And Tom and Mr Tucker looked at the barometer, and the weathercock, and got the logbook out and all that.

And me and Suzanne took Beatrice to the shed. And put the lock on. And made up a password. And I asked Suzanne if she thought Graham Roberts was right about Barney being dead.

"Because," I said, "even though Graham doesn't know about lots of things, like talking in French, and doing investigations, and Lifesaving, like we do, he might know more about sheep, and dogs, and farms and all that. Because of living on one."

Suzanne didn't answer. She got the list of things to do to help Beatrice out of her pocket. "We've done Number 1, and Number 2, and

Number 3. The next thing is Number 4: 'get another dog to keep your dog company.'"

So that's what we decided to do. Suzanne's Mum didn't look very pleased when Suzanne asked her if she could get another dog.

"Is this a *joke*?"

"No," Suzanne said. Because it was serious.

Suzanne's Mum pointed to the list of reasons on the fridge for why it was a good idea for the Barrys to get Suzanne's Mum's Aunt's dog. And the part where Suzanne had put that if they got the dog, she would never ask for anything else, and especially not another dog. And if she did they could give Beatrice back to Aunt Deidra's Nephew, Mick.

So me and Suzanne went to my house, to ask Mum if we could get a dog instead.

Mum wasn't pleased to see Beatrice, especially not in Mrs Rotherham's knickers. Because she said it wasn't polite to go asking old ladies for their pants, to put on your pets. And she had already told us we weren't allowed.

"We didn't ask," I said, which was true, "Mrs Rotherham offered." Mum still didn't look very pleased. So I waited for a bit. And then I said, *"Mum?"*

"Yes?"

"Can we get a dog, please, to keep Beatrice company, and be her friend, and stop her being depressed?"

"Ha!" Mum said. "If there is one thing that Beatrice has made clear, it is that we are never, *ever*, getting a dog."

So me and Suzanne went back to the shed to try to think of where we could find a dog for Beatrice to be friends with.

"What about Misty?" Suzanne said.

"I don't think Misty makes friends," I said. Because she just runs backwards and forwards behind Miss Matheson's fence all day, baring her teeth and yapping and snapping and attacking anyone who comes close.

"Some dogs get aggressive when they're guarding their homes," Suzanne said. Which is probably true. And some *people* do too, because whenever Miss Matheson sees us trying to get over her gate, she bangs on the window and says, **"PRIVATE PROPERTY, PRIVATE PROPERTY!"**

"Maybe if Beatrice just bumped into Misty, in the road, she might be more friendly."

So we decided that Beatrice and Misty should meet without me and Suzanne. Because Miss Matheson might not want Misty to be Beatrice's friend if we were there with her.

So we made a plan to sit in the shed and look through the spy hole and wait for Miss Matheson and Misty to come back from their morning walk.

We took the lock off the door, and got Beatrice in position in front of it. And I stood behind Beatrice, ready to push. And Suzanne looked through the spyhole. And we waited. And waited. And it started to rain. And then Suzanne said, "They're coming. Quick, Anna!"

Miss Matheson had picked Misty up, and

started to hurry. I gave Beatrice a push. And then I pushed her a bit harder. And then I got down, and wriggled my shoulder underneath Beatrice's bum, and pushed forward and up as hard as I could.

Beatrice snored.

"Now, before it's too late."

My arms shook. **"Nngnngya!"**

Beatrice's back end wobbled a bit. Then she went forward, and the shed door swung open, and she fell into the lane. Right at Miss Matheson's feet. Miss Matheson screamed, and threw her hands up in the air, and Misty went up in the air too. And Beatrice shook herself, and yawned, and then Misty came down. And Beatrice caught her, in her mouth. And then she spat Misty out. On the ground.

Beatrice nudged her with her nose, but Misty didn't move.

And Miss Matheson picked Misty up and hurried into her house, calling, **"HELP, HELP, POLICE!"**

And me and Suzanne got Beatrice back into the shed. And we put the lock on the door. And sat very still. And listened to the rain on the roof.

✌ CHAPTER 15 ✌
The Farm

There was a knock on the shed door. Suzanne looked through the spy hole.

"It's your Mum, Anna. And your Dad. And *my* Mum and Dad. And a *Policeman*."

"What's the password?" I asked.

"Open the door, Anna, please. There's a policeman to see you."

"That's not the password," I said.

"Where's his badge?" asked Suzanne. The Policeman held a police badge up to the spy hole. Suzanne looked at it. And she opened the door a crack.

The Policeman was standing in

front of it. "I understand there's been an incident, involving a Newfoundland and your neighbour's Chihuahua."

He looked round the door, into the shed, at Beatrice. "I take it this is the animal in question?"

Suzanne nodded. "Yes."

And the Policeman said we needed to tell him exactly what happened.

"You'd better come in," Suzanne said. And he did. And we told him all about how Beatrice was depressed, and showed him the list of things we were doing to help her, and how we were up to Number 4, which was to find her a dog companion. And the Policeman nodded, and wrote in his notebook.

And after a bit he said, "I'm going to just

step outside, if you don't mind. It's a bit tight in here." Which was true, because he was squashed in the corner, behind the door, because Beatrice took up most of the room. "And a bit ripe, too." Which was true as well. Because Beatrice's bath was wearing off, and her nappy was full, and we'd run out of extra strong mints.

So we all went into Suzanne's house. Apart from Beatrice. Because Suzanne's Dad put her in the garage. And the Policeman asked me and Suzanne lots of questions. About Beatrice. And Misty. And Miss Matheson. And what had happened. And we answered them. And told him all about our plan for Beatrice to meet Misty. And how I pushed her out into the lane. And how she landed in front of Miss Matheson.

And how Miss Matheson jumped, and threw her hands, and Misty, up in the air. And how Misty came back down and Beatrice caught Misty in her mouth.

"Is Misty going to be alright?" Suzanne asked.

"Time will tell. Punctured lung." He closed his notebook. And then he talked to Suzanne's Mum and Dad for a bit about Miss Matheson, and how she had reported Beatrice, and wanted to press charges against Suzanne's Mum and Dad. "There are a range of possible charges. From failure to control your dog in a public place, to setting or urging a dog to attack. And a range of penalties to accompany them. Worst case scenario, if it goes to court, is a fine of £5,000." And he said how Miss Matheson thought Beatrice was a dangerous dog, and needed to be put down.

"You're not going to have Beatrice *put down*, are you?" Suzanne asked.

Suzanne's Mum and Dad looked at each other. "No."

Then Suzanne's Dad said, "But it might be better if Beatrice went to live on the farm where Barney is, where she can run in the fields."

And Suzanne's Mum said, "She'll be better off."

CHAPTER 16
What Happened to Barney?

Me and Mum and Dad went home to have lunch.

"Mum?"

"Yes?"

"Where's Barney?"

"Urm, I think he went to live on a farm, isn't that what Suzanne's Dad said?"

"Where is it?"

"I'm not sure."

"What's it called?"

"I can't remember."

"I want to go and see him."

"Oh, I don't think so, Anna... It's too far away."

"Me and Suzanne could go on our bikes."

"It's too far for that. You'd have to go in a car."

"We could go on the bus."

"Buses don't go out that way."

"I thought you didn't know where it was?"

"I don't. Eat your broccoli."

I ate my broccoli. And went upstairs. And knocked three times on the wall. Suzanne knocked back. I opened the window. And stuck my head out. It was still raining. "Bonjour."

"Bonjour."

"It's wet."

"Anna, do you think Barney is dead?"

And I was going to say, "Non" (which is French for 'no'), because I knew Suzanne didn't want Barney to be dead, and because when Graham Roberts said he was, Suzanne pushed him. I waited a bit. And picked some of the paint off the window ledge. And then I said, "Yes. I think Barney's dead." Because I did. Suzanne didn't say anything. Because she cried, instead. And we stayed with our heads hanging out of the windows. And the rain soaked our hair and ran down our necks.

And then after ages Suzanne said, "Meet me at ze shed."

We put the lock on the door and made up a new password, which was "mort", because Suzanne said that's French for "dead". And Suzanne got a piece of paper, and she put 'Anna's and Suzanne's Investigation Into What Happened To Barney' on the top of it. And then she put:

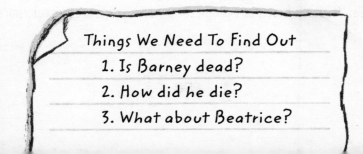

Things We Need To Find Out
1. Is Barney dead?
2. How did he die?
3. What about Beatrice?

And we made a plan.

Which was that Suzanne would go to her house and get her Mum and Dad into the front room, and keep them there as long as she could, asking questions about Barney, and the farm, and where it was, and why she couldn't visit. And I would sneak in the back, through the garage, and look for evidence. In case Suzanne's Mum and Dad didn't admit that Barney was dead. And when Suzanne couldn't keep her Mum and Dad in the front room any more she would cough, three times, to warn me to get out.

"Good plan," I said. And then I said, "What kind of evidence should I look for, exactly?"

And Suzanne said, "Every kind."

"Okay."

So Suzanne went round the front of her house. And I waited for a bit.

And then I walked down to sneak in through the Barrys' garage. And on the way, I looked along the flowerbeds in the lane, in case there was a big mound of earth, where Suzanne's Mum and Dad had buried Barney, out the back. Where our Old Cat is buried, and the nine hamsters, and Joe's old rabbit. But there wasn't.

I went in the Barrys' garage, and through the kitchen, and I snuck into Suzanne's Dad's office. Because that's the room Suzanne's Dad is always telling her to get out of. And I looked on Suzanne's Dad's desk. There was a photo of Suzanne's Mum and Dad, when they were married, and one of Carl, when he was just born, and one of Suzanne and Barney in the garden. There was a diary. I flicked through the pages in case it said, "killed Barney today" or something like that. But it didn't. I put it in my pocket anyway.

There was a big drawer in the desk with files in, with labels on, in order, saying 'Appliances', and 'Bank', and 'Car', and all that. And each file was full of papers, and letters, and bills. And Suzanne's Dad had written 'PAID' across some of them, in big red letters. I looked along the line of files in case there was one that said 'Barney', or 'Beatrice', or 'Dogs'.

Then I heard Suzanne. "Eh hem, eh hem, eh *hem*." It was the three warning coughs.

I flicked through the files quickly. Until I came to the last one. It said 'Vet'.

"EH HEM, EH HEM, EH HEM."

I shoved the file up my jumper, and sneaked back out of the office, and through the kitchen and the garage, back to the shed. And waited for Suzanne.

There were three knocks on the door. "Mort." I opened it.

"They didn't admit *anything*," Suzanne said. "What evidence did you get?"

I passed Suzanne the diary and the Vet file. She opened it. There were two bills for Beatrice inside, one which said abscess lancing, ear wax removal, antibiotic injection, worming pill. Cost: £150. Which was all the things Beatrice had had done the day me and Suzanne and Suzanne's Mum took her to the Vet's. And there was another bill which said tumour biopsies, tooth extraction, teeth scaling, gastric probe, MRI scan, bladder lifting surgery, vaccinations. Estimated cost: £1500. Which was for all the things she hadn't had done yet. And then there were lots of bills for Barney for having his teeth scaled, and his toenails clipped, and vaccinations, and worming, and one that said brain tumour biopsy. And they all had 'PAID' and a date written across them. And the last bill in the file said 'Euthanasia for dog: £65.' Suzanne looked at the bill. It had a date on the top: Friday 26th June. And she got her Dad's diary, and flicked back through the pages.

"Friday the 26th of June. Anna, *look*."

At the top of the page in the diary her Dad had written: **Barney to Farm.**

Suzanne passed me the dictionary. This is what it says about Euthanasia:

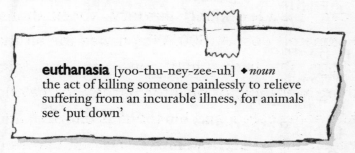

euthanasia [yoo-thu-ney-zee-uh] ◆ *noun*
the act of killing someone painlessly to relieve suffering from an incurable illness, for animals see 'put down'

We looked again at Barney's euthanasia bill. It had 'PAID' written across it, in big red letters. Suzanne picked her dad's diary up and started flicking through it again. She pointed to a date. "Monday 27th September. That's tomorrow's date. Look, Anna." It said: **9.45, Beatrice to Farm.**

ANNA'S AND SUZANNE'S LIST OF THINGS WE NEED FOR OUR PLAN TO HELP BEATRICE ESCAPE

- ☐ Beatrice
- ☐ Tom
- ☐ Tom's dinghy
- ☐ Mrs Rotherham's black sheepskin rug
- ☐ The Lifesavers' practice rope
- ☐ Dog food
- ☐ Bottle of water
- ☐ Anna's and Suzanne's lunch boxes
- ☐ Rucksack

Tom was sitting in the dinghy, in the hall, with Batman, and Bob the Builder, and his two slugs from Sunday School. I told him about Barney, how he wasn't on a farm, roaming free where he was better off, because Suzanne's Mum and Dad had had him euthanised.

"What's that?"

"Put down"

"What's that?"

"Dead."

"Oh," Tom said. "Who killed him?"

"The Vet."

"Why?"

"Because Suzanne's Mum and Dad asked her to."

"Why?"

"It doesn't matter," I said. Because once Tom

starts asking why, he won't stop. And we didn't have much time to do the plan to help Beatrice escape. And I told him how he had to come with us to the shed because he was on our list of things for our plan to save Beatrice. And how we needed his dinghy as well.

"It's not a dinghy, it's an ark."

"Your ark, then."

But Tom said he didn't have time because he had to get his ark ready before the flood came up.

"I'll get you some biscuits," Suzanne said. So Tom said he would come. And Suzanne went to her house, and pinched him some biscuits.

And Tom took them, and picked up the

166

dinghy and said, "But when the flood comes it's just for me, and Batman and Bob the Builder, and my slugs. Because there's not much room. And I've got to leave space for The New Cat, and Mr Tucker, and my biscuits."

So we took Tom's ark to the shed. And then we went to get Mrs Rotherham's rug. Mrs Rotherham didn't really want to give us her rug. Because she said, "Why?" And we said how it was for Beatrice to sleep with tonight because tomorrow she was going to live on the farm, like Barney, and we wanted her to have a comfortable last night.

"I'm all for comfort," Mrs Rotherham said. And she gave us a big carrier bag to put it in, so it didn't get wet.

And then we went back to the shed and we put the rug in a rucksack, with the practice rescue rope, from Lifesavers, and the lunch boxes packed with dog food, and the water. And we put a new nappy in Beatrice's pants. And got our coats on, and our wellies. And Suzanne ticked each thing off on the list.

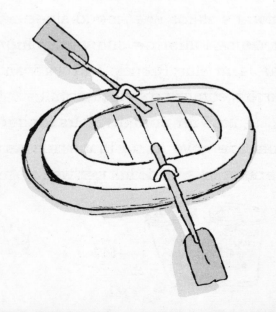

CHAPTER 17
Beatrice Escapes

Suzanne clipped the lead onto Beatrice's collar.

"Walkies."

Beatrice got up. Without me having to get underneath her to lever her up.

And me and Suzanne and Tom and Beatrice started walking down the back lane, in the rain. And we didn't push and pull, and stop and start, all the way like we normally do. Because Beatrice just walked, like other dogs do. And Suzanne said she thought that Beatrice must know that she was meant to be getting put down tomorrow. And maybe she was *psychic*. Which she said means she could see what was going to happen in the future. Because she said, "some dogs *are*." Because she saw a programme all about it, on telly called 'Telepathic Pets'. And I said I thought that was probably why Beatrice was so much faster. And also because the wind was blowing behind us. And it was so strong that Tom couldn't hold onto the dinghy, and we had to tie it onto Suzanne's rucksack, so we didn't lose it. And the wind kept getting under it, and Tom kept getting blown forwards. And the rain got heavier.

Down in the village people were running to get indoors, and someone's umbrella had blown inside out. And the sweet shop lady was chasing her ice cream sign that had blown into the road.

We came to the bridge. And turned right, down to the river, and the path down was so wet that it was hard to stay standing up, and Tom had to slide down on his bum. Down on the riverbank we walked close together, with the dinghy over our heads, to keep the rain off. Apart from Beatrice. Who walked ahead. And had her tail wagging, and her nose up.

"Beatrice likes the rain," Tom said.

We stopped at Aunt Deidra's cottage, and Suzanne climbed over the gate, and opened it and let me and Tom and Beatrice inside. And we walked up the garden, to the top, and Suzanne unclipped Beatrice's lead, and took the cone off her neck. And we got our packed lunch boxes out. And put them down in front of the kennel. And Suzanne poured the dog food into hers. And I poured the water into mine. And I put Beatrice's cone round Tom's neck, and clipped her lead onto his coat. And we put the dinghy on his back, upside down, and Mrs Rotherham's black sheepskin rug over, to cover it, and Tom held the handles. And in the dark, and the wind, and the rain, if you half closed your eyes, he looked *exactly* like Beatrice. And Suzanne tied one end of

the practice rope to Beatrice's collar, and the other end to a ring in the ground, next to Beatrice's kennel.

And Suzanne said we should each give Beatrice a hug, and say something nice, to keep her going through the night with affection, so she didn't get depressed again.

And I said, "Beatrice, I'm glad you aren't going to get put down."

And Suzanne said, "You are the best dog I have ever had. Apart from Barney."

And Tom said, "You are too big to get in my ark."

And we told Beatrice we would be back in the morning, before school, with some fresh water and some more food. And we said goodbye. And walked back down the garden.

And turned right out of the gate, and went up over the field. And the wind kept trying to blow the dinghy off Tom's back. And me and Suzanne had to hold it on. And the rain collected in Beatrice's cone around Tom's neck. And we kept having to stop, to empty it out, and to wring Mrs Rotherham's rug out as well.

We got onto the road that leads back to the village, and there wasn't anyone out, because they had all gone indoors. And it was as dark as if it was the middle of the night. And then there was thunder. And it sounded like when our class went on a trip to the fort, and they fired the hundred tonne gun.

And we ran until we came to the bottom of our road.

Mr Tucker was coming down it. "Popsie,

Blondie, that you?"

"Yes."

"Where's Basher?"

Suzanne nudged Tom.

"Here," Tom said, from under the dinghy.

"Can't see a thing in these specs in this weather. Thought you were the dog, Basher. Better get inside. Mum's out looking for you." He did the salute. "Into the old ark, eh?"

We went up the back lane. Suzanne's Mum banged on the kitchen window, **"WHERE HAVE YOU BEEN?"**

"Taking Beatrice for her walk," Suzanne said. And her Mum wasn't pleased because she said Suzanne's Dad was out looking for us all in the car.

We went into the garage, and Suzanne took

Beatrice's cone and lead off Tom, and put them in the rucksack, and we wrung out Mrs Rotherham's rug, over the drain, and and ran out to the shed with it, and hung it over the ladders, at the back, to dry.

And me and Tom took the dinghy home. And we'd just got in when Mum came in the front door. And she was very wet and she wasn't very pleased because she said she thought we were all in the shed. And we had no business going for a walk without telling her, and especially not in a storm. And Tom told her how it was fine because he had his ark with him and all that. And me and Tom had a bath, and our tea.

And I knocked on the wall, and Suzanne knocked back, and we tried to put our heads out, but it was raining so hard that the rain came in sideways through the gap and it was so loud that we couldn't hear each other speak. So we went back in, and went to bed. And Tom came and slept in my room. Because he didn't like the noise of the storm. And he brought his ark with him. And we talked about Beatrice a bit and listened to the thunder.

And we didn't hear anything else until the morning when Suzanne's Dad said, **"WHERE ON EARTH IS THAT DAMNED DOG?!"**

CHAPTER 18

The Rain Came Down

Mum came into my room. "Suzanne's Dad is going to drive you all to school this morning."

"I want to walk."

"Don't be ridiculous, Anna, you're not walking. Have you seen it outside?"

I looked out the window. It was raining harder than ever. I waited until Mum had gone, and I knocked three times on the wall. Suzanne knocked back, and we opened our windows. And stuck our heads out. And then we brought them back in again, because it was so heavy that you couldn't keep your eyes open, and it hurt your ears, and you couldn't speak.

I shouted through the window, "What are we going to do?" Because we were supposed to set off for school early, to go down to see Beatrice, and check she was alright, and take her some food.

"We could sneak out of school at lunch time," Suzanne said, "and go and see Beatrice and get back before the bell goes. I'll bring the dog food to school."

But at lunchtime Mrs Peters said it was wet play, and everyone had to stay inside. And the rain kept on coming. And in the afternoon the people who come in to school on buses, and live out of the village, got sent home early because the rain was getting worse, and if they waited they might not get through.

When the bell went for home time, Suzanne's Mum was waiting for us at the gates in her car.

When we got home I tried to sneak out to meet Suzanne in the shed. But Mum saw me. "Don't be ridiculous, Anna. The shed's half full of water. I've been in there today and put buckets under all the leaks. What on earth was that sopping wet rug doing there?"

After tea the rain still hadn't stopped. And it kept raining all through the night. Because I could hear it, in bed, and I couldn't sleep because it was so loud, and I kept thinking about Beatrice, and Suzanne, and whether Beatrice was alright, and how she would need a new nappy in, and whether her food had run out.

 CHAPTER 19

The Floods Came Up

In the morning, when I woke up, and went downstairs, Tom was already up and dressed and sitting in the hall in the dinghy.

"The flood has come," he said.

"No it hasn't."

"It has. Ask Mum."

I looked out of the window. The rain had stopped. Mum had the news on.

"Tom says the flood's come."

"Shh, Anna," Mum said, pointing to the telly. "Look."

There was a man on the telly standing by the bridge in the village. "That's right, Carol,

181

I'm here on the north side of the bridge, and, as you can see behind me, over there on the south side, the river has already burst its banks. Many people on the south side were evacuated in the night and with severe weather warnings again for this afternoon and this evening, police are now advising people living close to the river on the north side to move to higher ground as well. Schools in the immediate area are closed…"

I ran upstairs and knocked on the wall three times, and Suzanne knocked back, and

I opened my window and stuck my head out, and Suzanne opened hers.

"We have to evacuate Beatrice and move her to higher ground."

I got dressed and ran downstairs,

"Where are you going?"

"To look at the flood."

Tom was still in the hall sitting in the dinghy. "I'm coming." And he picked up the dinghy by the string. And his packet of biscuits.

Mum shouted after us, "Stay where everyone else is, Anna. And don't go down near the water!"

☀ CHAPTER 20 ☀

The River

We couldn't get to Sorrel Cottage by going past the shops, and turning right before the bridge, like we normally do. Because everyone was out in the village, looking at the river, and filming the flood. So we walked along the back road behind the church, and down over the fields instead. And the grass was so wet that we could pull Tom along behind us, in the dinghy.

As we got closer we could hear the river getting louder. And down on the riverbank it was so loud Tom put his hands over his ears. We stopped and stared at the river.

"It's gone big," Tom said.

And it had. Because the fields on the other side of the river had all disappeared underneath it. And the island in the middle was missing. And you could just see the highest branches of the trees, sticking out the top.

"I don't like it," Tom said. And he started eating his biscuits.

I didn't like it either. Because the water was so fast, it went past white, and swirled round in rapids, and there were waves under the bridge. And looking at it made me feel a bit sick.

We carried on along the riverbank until we came to Sorrel Cottage. Suzanne looked over the gate. "There she *is.*"

Beatrice was lying in a puddle, next to the kennel, at the top of the garden.

"Beatrice!" Suzanne climbed over the gate, and opened it from the inside. Beatrice stood up. And wagged her tail. And barked. Like a proper dog. Me and Suzanne walked up to meet her.

Tom stayed with the dinghy, on the river bank and stared at the river and ate his biscuits.

Beatrice was as wet as Mrs Rotherham's black rug, the night it got soaked in the storm. Suzanne put her arms around Beatrice. And Beatrice rubbed her face against Suzanne, like she was Great Aunt Deidra's gate. I could hear the river, at the top of the garden. And then I heard another noise. **"Quack."**

"What was that?"

"What?"

"I heard something."

"Quack."

I turned around. There were three ducks on the other side of Aunt Deidra's gate, waddling towards Tom.

"Shoo," Tom shouted. "Go away." He took a step backwards toward the river, with the string of the dinghy in one hand, and his packet of biscuits in the other. Three more ducks came out from in the gorse bushes.

"Quack"

"On your left, Tom."

"Quack."

"And your right."

"Shoo." Tom took another step back. And

waved his biscuits. And the ducks started coming towards him all together, opening their beaks, and flapping their wings.

"Throw the biscuits, Tom!"

But Tom didn't. He just kept walking away. Backwards. Towards the river.

I ran down the garden, and through the gate. Tom was nearly at the edge of the riverbank.

"HONK!"

Tom jumped. "What was that?"

The Swan Duck pushed its way through the others to the front. It looked at Tom, and his biscuits, with its good eye. And the white eye, that looks off the wrong way, looked behind it. Then it reared up, and stuck out its chest, and opened its wings, then hissed, **"TSSSSS!"**

It ran at Tom, and the ducks followed behind

it, hissing and pecking and flapping like mad. Tom was right at the edge of the riverbank now. He looked behind him. **"HELP!"**

I could hear the river, loud, like when the trains go over at the crossing.

And suddenly the bank gave way, and Tom disappeared into the river, and shot down it, holding onto the dinghy.

"Tom! Hold on!"

Tom grabbed onto a branch of a tree, which was sticking out of the water where the island used to be. He let go of the dinghy and it shot off through the rapids.

"My ark!"

On the bridge, people started pointing. "There's a boy!", "Look!", "Somebody do

something!"

"The rope..." I shouted to Suzanne.

Suzanne started trying to untie the rope from Beatrice's collar.

"It's too wet!" Suzanne called. "I can't undo the knot!"

She ran down from the top of the garden, and through the gate, and over the riverbank. "I'll dive in, Anna, stand back!" She took her boots off and put her arms up over her head. But before she could dive in, Beatrice did something she had never done. She ran. She ran so hard that the ring with the rope on came out of the ground, and she dragged it behind her. She dived into the water, in front of Suzanne, and swam across the current. And stopped just in front of Tom. They both went under. And I thought they had both drowned. Because I counted thirty. Which is the longest Tom has ever held his breath. And then they came up back up, above the water, and Beatrice had the hood of Tom's jacket in her mouth. And she dragged him back to the riverbank.

THE RESCUE
- how it Happened...

NEWS

BRIDGE

me

Suzanne

BEATRICE!!

Rope
- Failed!

RAPIDS

BRANCH

DINGHY

FLOOD

Tom

CHAPTER 21

In The News

Two ambulance men came, and wrapped Tom in a silver blanket, and put an oxygen mask on him, and put him on a stretcher. And people from up on the bridge, who had seen what happened, ran down, and gathered round. And one of the ambulance men tapped Tom on the cheek, "Can you hear me?"

And Tom could. Because he nodded his head.

And the ambulance men asked Tom some questions. About who he was and where he lived and all that, and shone a little torch in his eyes. And Tom couldn't answer because his

teeth were chattering so much, and his lips
had gone blue, and then he was sick. And he
started crying because he'd lost his ark, and
his biscuits. And there was a lady from the
paper trying to ask questions too. And I said
how Tom was my brother. And the lady from
the paper started asking me questions instead.
And I told her how we had come to have a look

at the flood. And how Tom got attacked by the ducks. And how Beatrice was Suzanne's dog, and she'd gone missing, on Monday. And I started to say how Beatrice had nearly killed Misty by mistake, and Miss Matheson wanted to take her to court, and Suzanne's Dad was going to have her put down.

But Suzanne kicked me in the shin, and put her eyebrows up, and made her lips go small, like she does when she wants you to shut up.

And then I saw Mum and Dad running down the riverbank, and Suzanne's Mum and Dad as well. And they had seen everything, on the news. And Mum and Dad went with Tom in the ambulance. And Suzanne's Dad asked the lady who she was. And the lady from the paper tried to give Suzanne's Dad her card, in case he would like to tell her his story.

And Suzanne's Dad said, "No thanks."

And the lady shook my hand, and put a card in it, and went off. And we all went up home.

The next day a big picture of Beatrice was on the front page of the paper.

THE DEADLY CURRENTS OF A FLOODED RIVER PROVED NO MATCH FOR THE LOVE OF A DEVOTED FAMILY PET WHEN A DOG CAME TO THE RESCUE OF A DROWNING CHILD.

Anna Morris (9) and her brother Tom (5) and their friend and next-door-neighbour Suzanne Barry had a brush with tragedy yesterday morning as a section of riverbank collapsed, plunging the five-year-old boy into the raging river. Eyewitnesses were incredulous at the sight of Beatrice, an aged Newfoundland, diving in and dragging the helpless child out of the water. The dog which was recently bequeathed to the Barry family following the death of an elderly Aunt, had gone missing the previous day. "Beatrice appeared from nowhere," Suzanne Barry said, "I was about to dive into the river, to rescue Tom, when Beatrice went in first."

I knocked on the wall three times. Suzanne knocked back. We opened our windows,

"Look!" And I showed Suzanne the paper. Suzanne didn't look pleased. "Don't you like it? Beatrice is a hero."

And Suzanne said how it didn't matter that Beatrice was a hero because her Mum and Dad had explained everything to her about Barney, and what was wrong with him, and how he'd had to be put down. And how they had to think about how old Beatrice was, and how much the Vet's bills would cost. And how even though Misty was starting to get better, if the Barrys didn't have Beatrice put down, Miss Matheson was still going to press charges, and they couldn't afford the fine. And if they lost the case they might have to cover Miss

Matheson's court costs.

"Want to come in the shed, and make a plan?" I said. "Because we could put all our pocket money together. And . . ."

But Suzanne didn't want to come in the shed. And she closed the window and went inside.

So I went out to the shed myself. And I got the buckets of water that Mum had put under the leaks and I emptied them out in the back lane. And I got Mrs Rotherham's rug and I went up the road to take it back.

And I showed Mrs Rotherham the paper, and the photo of Beatrice. And I told her all about how Beatrice wasn't well, and how she needed lots of things doing at the Vet's, and how she was too old, and it was too expensive. And how she had nearly killed Misty, by mistake.

And how Miss Matheson wanted her to be put down. Because Miss Matheson said she was a dangerous dog. And how she was going to take the Barrys to court. And I said how we couldn't get enough money to help because even if me and Suzanne sold everything we owned and did stalls at the bottom of the road and gave all our pocket money, we still wouldn't have enough because it would cost hundreds and maybe even thousands of pounds.

And Mrs Rotherham listened, and looked at the pictures in the paper. And said, "Well, well, well," and "dear, oh dear," and "Poor old Beatrice." And she started flicking through the pages, like she was looking for something. "Ah ha! Here it is." She pointed to a bit on the back page.

Got a story?

From celebrity exclusives to cheating politicians, to heartwarming tales of triumph over tragedy, we want your stories on all of them. Find out how much **YOU** could make: call us now.

I wasn't sure if Suzanne would want me to call the newspaper. Because when I was talking to the lady on the riverbank, Suzanne didn't like it. And nor did her Dad. And then I saw something else, under the phone number to call. 'You can remain anonymous. We always protect our sources.'

Mrs Rotherham passed me the phone.

The next day Beatrice was in the paper again.

HOW BEATRICE THE HERO DOG SUFFERS IN SILENCE.

Beatrice, who saved a five-year-old boy from drowning this week, has suffered with depression and has a list of health problems as long as your arm, but can't afford the medical care she needs…

And the day after that…

HERO DOG'S CHEQUERED HISTORY

Hours before she saved a small child from drowning, Beatrice the Newfoundland punctured the lung of a neighbour's chihuahua. A source close to Beatrice maintains this was a freak accident. But Miss Matheson, the owner of the pampered pooch, Misty, is determined to have the dog destroyed. A solicitor we spoke to commented, "Beatrice would more than likely get away with going to training classes. But the family may not feel able to take the risk of a ruling against her – then they'll be stuck with a large fine and court costs."

Beatrice was in the paper every day that week.

At the end of the week Suzanne knocked three times on the wall. And I knocked back. And we

said "Bonjour", and all that.

And Suzanne said, "Meet me at ze shed." Because she had something important to tell me.

So I did. And she said how she had been sent five cheques, for £200 each, from 'A well -wisher' to pay for Beatrice's Vet's bills. And how since Beatrice had been in the paper, people kept calling her house, like a solicitor who said that he would represent Beatrice for free. And a policeman who said Beatrice had been nominated for a Commendation of Bravery award. And the Vet, who said that she would knock some money off Beatrice's Vet's bills. And how Beatrice wasn't going to have to be put down.

CHAPTER 22
Life in the Old Dog Yet

That's pretty much everything that happened in the Great Dog Disaster. Me and Suzanne still take Beatrice for two walks every day. But not always down to Great Aunt Deidra's. Because we go all over the village. And Tom comes too. And the walks are slower than ever. Because, even though Beatrice isn't depressed anymore, and she can walk a bit faster, everyone we pass stops to give her a pat, and to look at her medal, and say, "Life in the old dog yet..." and all that. And Tom has to tell them the story of how Beatrice saved his life, after the ducks tried to drown him.

And on Mondays, when me and Suzanne go

to Lifesavers, Suzanne's Mum takes Beatrice to her *own* swimming lesson, in a special place, just for dogs, down the road from mine and Suzanne's, called Hydrotherapy Hounds. To help with her hips. And that's Beatrice's best thing of the week. And it's mine and Suzanne's as well. Because when we've finished our lesson, we watch Beatrice do hers through the window. And Beatrice doesn't look old at all in the water. And Suzanne says that, one day, Beatrice might start jumping up, and fetching a stick, and doing the obstacle course and all that. But I don't think so. Because mainly Beatrice likes to go and see Mrs Rotherham, and sit by her fire. And to have a bath, in the back lane on Sundays. And to fall asleep in the shed, while me and Suzanne make plans.

Katie Davies

Katie Davies was born in Newcastle Upon Tyne in 1978. In 1989, after a relentless begging campaign, she was given two hamsters for Christmas. She is yet to recover from what happened to those hamsters. THE GREAT HAMSTER MASSACRE, Katie's first novel, won the Waterstone's Children's Book Prize. She has also written THE GREAT RABBIT RESCUE, and THE GREAT CAT CONSPIRACY. Katie now lives in North London with her husband, the comedian Alan Davies, and their two small children. She does not have any hamsters.

Hannah Shaw

Hannah Shaw was born into a large family of sprout-munching vegetarians. She spent her formative years trying to be good at everything from roller-skating to gymnastics, but she soon realised there wasn't much chance of her becoming a gold medal-winning gymnast, so she resigned herself to writing stories and drawing pictures instead!

Hannah currently lives in the Cotswolds with her husband Ben the blacksmith and her rescue dog Ren. Hannah and Ren do dog agility together and they have a growing collection of 'special' and 'good effort' rosettes. She finds her over-active imagination fuels new ideas but unfortunately keeps her awake at night!

www.katiedaviesbooks.com

Visit Katie Davies online and find
out more amazing animal facts,
fun activities and exclusive news...